D0232782

PACIFIC RIM
UPRISING

THE JUNIOR NOVEL

ADAPTED BY
BECKY MATHESON

INSIGHT
EDITIONS
San Rafael, California

**INSIGHT
EDITIONS**

PO Box 3088
San Rafael, CA 94912
www.insighteditions.com

 Find us on Facebook: www.facebook.com/InsightEditions
 Follow us on Twitter: @insighteditions

Library of Congress Cataloging-in-Publication Data available.

ISBN: 978-1-68383-386-4

Publisher: Raoul Goff
Associate Publisher: Vanessa Lopez
Art Director: Chrissy Kwasnik
Designer: Evelyn Furuta
Editors: Erum Khan and Hilary VandenBroek
Editorial Assistant: Kaia Waller
Production Editor: Lauren LePera
Production Manager: Sam Taylor

ROOTS of PEACE REPLANTED PAPER

Insight Editions, in association with Roots of Peace, will plant two trees for each tree used in the
manufacturing of this book. Roots of Peace is an internationally renowned humanitarian organization
dedicated to eradicating land mines worldwide and converting war-torn lands into productive farms
and wildlife habitats. Roots of Peace will plant two million fruit and nut trees in Afghanistan and
provide farmers there with the skills and support necessary for sustainable land use.

Manufactured in the United States by Insight Editions

10 9 8 7 6 5 4 3 2 1

THE JUNIOR NOVEL

*E*arth. *Looks pretty from out here, doesn't it? All blue and shiny and happy. But get up close, and it all falls apart. My generation, we were born into war. Into a world of chaos.*

Something called the Breach opened up at the bottom of the Pacific Ocean. A gateway to another dimension. Sounds cool, doesn't it? Except on the other side is an alien race called the Precursors. They thought it'd be a laugh to send giant monsters through the Breach to say hello. We called those monsters Kaiju.

To fight them, we built our own monsters: Jaegers.

Jaegers were big bad metal machines—so big they needed two pilots to run them, with their minds connected together in the Drift.

Ten years ago, we sealed the Breach. We won the war.

But you wouldn't know it by looking around. The Kaiju made every hit count. Coastal cities got it the worst. Now the relief zones are filled with folks just trying to get by, psycho cults that worship the Kaiju like they are gods or something, and homegrown gangsters slapping together their own junk Jaegers from stolen parts.

Anyone with money moved inland. Middle of Nowhere became the new Beverly Hills. Because everybody's afraid of another breach opening up. Afraid of another Kaiju attack.

Which is cool with me. Because one man's fear is another man's opportunity. In the relief zones, you have to get creative. Out here, we place a different value on things. The Pan Pacific Defense Corps usually looks the other way—as long as you don't go poking around where you don't belong.

. . . Say, like a scrapyard of decommissioned Jaegers. But laying hands on their Jaeger tech is worth the risk. Good score will set you up for a year. And I got a knack for delivering for my customers . . .

. . . Most of the time.

Darkness engulfed the scrapyard, but Jake didn't have to see the ground to know where he was going. It was all familiar to him at this point—the electric fence that sparked and hummed, the hole ripped into it that he could easily crawl through, and most of all, the fallen Jaeger bodies with their metal body parts littering the ground. Jake pulled out the plasma tracker from his jacket. He could feel Sonny and his men right behind him.

He quickly put his arm up to stop Sonny from walking forward. A PPDC security vehicle rumbled by. Jake shot Sonny a warning look. The area was heavily patrolled, and they needed to be careful. Suddenly, his plasma tracker pinged. Jake looked up at the remains of the Jaeger in front of them and smiled. He knew it would be here.

He yanked on the hidden release inside the panel, and grinned as the access door opened.

But the second he was inside, he knew something was wrong. Cables hung down from the ceiling. Electricity sparked at their ends. The plasma capacitor was gone!

CRACK! Sonny whipped Jake in the face with his handgun. Jake fell to the ground. The sting pulsed through his whole body.

"Kill him," said Sonny, turning to leave.

Jake thumped his tracker and the screen flickered. It showed that the plasma capacitor was on the move. Somebody else was in there, and they had it.

He jumped up, quickly scrambling over the machine parts. He slipped through the doorway. One of Sonny's men caught up to him, and Jake quickly laid him out. Then, he ran full tilt through the corridors.

He followed the signal on the tracker. He knew every inch of this scrapyard, but he also knew that if Sonny and his men caught him, this time they wouldn't hesitate to kill him. He dashed into a tunnel thick with power cables. He made his way through them, left and right until he was clear of the scrapyard.

Dawn was breaking over Santa Monica, California, as Jake ran. Sunrays gleamed against the broken-down machinery, dirty streets, and slums of a city that had once been beautiful. Now, it was a wasteland inhabited by those too poor to move away from the water. If the Kaiju attacked again, the homes on the coast would be the first destroyed.

Jake's tracker pinged. He dashed up a hill of rubble and eyed the massive Kaiju bones that jutted out of the partially destroyed pier. His tracker locked onto an old shipyard down by the water. Gotcha!

Jake climbed into a grime-filled window and entered a building inside the shipyard. He looked at the room around him. There was a dirty mattress in the corner and food wrappers littered the floor, but the space was mostly full of junky old machine parts. The walls were plastered with images of Jaegers and Kaiju. Whoever lived here also had a thing for Shao Liwen. Clippings on the wall tracked her career from young computer genius to the head of the multibillion dollar company named after her: Shao Industries.

Jake's eyes fell on a faded *Time* magazine cover with Raleigh Becket's face on it, and the years of his birth and death: 1998–2026. Jake stopped the sadness from rising in his chest. He was here for a reason.

He reached the main floor. There, in the middle of the room, was some kind of machine. It looked like a . . . like a homemade Jaeger. It was nearly four stories tall and cobbled together with mismatched parts. Jake's tracker pinged loudly. Nestled in a hatch on the mini Jaeger's computer, the plasma capacitor caught his eye. But Jake couldn't think about that anymore—this little machine could be the real score! If he broke this little Jaeger down and sold off the parts, he'd have enough money to stop scrounging through scrapyards for good. He'd never have to deal with people like Sonny again.

Suddenly, a hooded figure jumped out from the shadows and swung a pipe at him. Jake wrenched the pipe away and slammed the figure into the ground. He raised the pipe and almost swung, but then stopped short.

"What! How old are you?" he stammered.

The figure pulled the hood back—revealing a fifteen-year-old girl.

"Old enough to kick your ass," said Amara. She started to get up but Jake nudged her back to the ground with the pipe.

"Let's take a minute. You build this thing yourself?"

"No, I gave my staff the day off. What do you think?"

"I think I could sell your toy for a whole lot of money," said Jake.

"Scrapper's not a toy, and she's not for sale!" Amara shot back.

"The man holding the pipe says she is, so—"

A siren screamed through the air.

"You led *them* here?" Amara asked.

"What? Nobody follows me! It must have been you."

Jake looked toward the sound of the sirens. Amara kicked the pipe out of his hand. Then she kicked the plasma capacitor hatch closed and scrambled up Scrapper's leg.

PPDC vehicles swarmed the shipyard warehouse. Jake looked at the young girl and her makeshift Jaeger, then back at the vehicles. It was time to either take a gamble on this stranger who was clearly out of her mind, or stay and get arrested by the PPDC.

Amara connected into a gyroscopic cradle and powered the Jaeger up. Jake scrambled into the conn-pod just as Scrapper's chest plates slammed shut.

"Hey! Get out!" she screamed.

"Where's the other one?" asked Jake, confused.

"The other what?"

"The other cradle! Jaegers need two pilots!"

"Scrapper is small enough to run on a single neural load."

"Then move over and let me pilot!"

"No way!" Amara punched another key.

Boom! Scrapper smashed out of the warehouse.

"Woo! Told you she's not a toy!" Amara beamed.

"You're gonna get us hurt. Now, come on!" said Jake. He tried to uncouple her from the gyroscope.

"Stop it!" she warned.

"I can get us out of here," said Jake.

"I just got us out! Get off! Hey!"

Something appeared on the display. It was November Ajax! The Jaeger loomed over Scrapper, blocking out the sun. Amara looked up with respect and awe.

A voice boomed over the speaker: "Pilots of unregistered Jaeger. This is the Pan Pacific Defense Corps. Power down and exit your conn-pod."

Amara raised her hand in apparent surrender.

"That's it? You give up way too easy kid," said Jake.

"That's what they think." Amara clenched her fists. Smoke canisters shot out of Scrapper's arms. The smoke engulfed November Ajax's feet, so that the giant Jaeger couldn't see Scrapper beneath the smoke.

Whoosh! Scrapper barreled out of the smoke and took off down the street. Jake grabbed hold of a cable to balance himself.

November Ajax turned. He needed only one step to catch up to Scrapper.

"Hang on!" Amara shouted. She touched a final command, and the world spiraled around Jake.

Scrapper had curled into a ball! She crisscrossed between Ajax's feet, confusing the mighty Jaeger.

Jake jammed himself in the alcove to keep from getting tumbled. He couldn't help but be impressed at what this girl had engineered. Scrapper was doing these moves on a single neural load! The little Jaeger careened off palm trees and burned out cars. She rolled up the side of a pile of rubble, flew into the air, and crashed back down the wall of a collapsed building.

"See? I just out-piloted November Ajax," said Amara.

"You didn't," Jake smirked.

"Did!"

Boom! November Ajax's giant hand peeled back a wall of the collapsed building.

"Okay. What do you got?" said Amara. "And I'm not getting out!"

Jake looked around the conn-pod. He rushed over to the set of twin ion cells on the wall.

"One of these ion cells redundant?" he asked.

"No," said Amara.

Jake primed the eject sequence.

"Is now. Get us close to Ajax's head. Go!"

Amara shot Jake a dirty look, but she hit the gas. Scrapper scrambled up November Ajax's arm and over the metal Goliath's head. Jake ejected the ion cell. It bounced off November Ajax's head and ruptured! A mini electrical storm surged above Ajax. This would disrupt his systems alright.

Scrapper darted through the Santa Monica slums. The little Jaeger jumped onto the rooftop of an abandoned building, but the structure was old and weak. The roof collapsed under Scrapper's weight, and Scrapper fell into the building. Scrapper ran full tilt and smashed through the walls in front of her. Then a warning flashed on the display: RESERVE POWER AT 12%.

"Told you we needed that!" said Amara.

"It worked, didn't it?" Jake said, refusing to admit it was risky.

"How long before Ajax can reboot his systems?" she asked.

Thoom! November Ajax's foot crashed down into the building. Scrapper's path was blocked by a shower of sand!

"About that long," said Jake.

A voice boomed over November Ajax's loudspeakers: "Power down and exit your conn-pod. This is your final warning."

Amara wasn't about to give up. Scrapper turned and ran.

November Ajax raised a fist and cables shot out from its knuckle. Grapple hooks latched onto the little Jaeger, and an electric pulse surged through the cable. Scrapper convulsed. Her circuits fried. Smoke rose from the top of her head.

When the hatch slammed open, Jake walked out first. He shot a sour look up at November Ajax and raised his hands in the air. Amara followed. "Look what you did to my Jaeger!" she screamed up angrily.

Inside the holding cell, Jake and Amara waited for the PPDC. A tense silence grew between them.

"Should've let me pilot," Jake said.

"Like this is *my* fault?" She looked bewildered. "You compromised my command center!"

"Command center?" mocked Jake. "I'm not talking to you." Jake bit down on his cheek. The silence grew heavier. He couldn't help it. He had to know more.

"Why'd you build it?" he asked.

"What happened to the not talking?"

"Said you weren't going to sell it, so what? Rob a bank or something?"

Amara gave Jake a hard look. "I built her because one day they're gonna come back. The Kaiju. And when they do, I'm not gonna be stuck waiting for someone else to come save me. Not like before."

Jake considered the answer. It wasn't what he expected to hear. He studied Amara, but before he could ask anything else, two PPDC officers walked into the cell.

"You. Let's go." They grabbed Jake.

The two officers roughly shoved Jake into an interrogation room and slammed the door shut behind him. His eyes swept over his surroundings—nothing but an empty interrogation table. Then, holo emitters flared to life.

There, in colorful pixels dusted across the air, was Mako Mori. She was secretary-general of the PPDC now. Her hologram sat at the far end of the table.

Jake grinned in relief.

"There she is! My sister from another mister! You make some calls, pull some strings, I gotta sign some paperwork?" he asked.

"I was really hoping to not see you like this again," answered Mako.

Jake shrugged. "Just a stretch of bad luck, I'll figure it out."

"Father used to say we make our own luck," said Mako.

"Yeah, dad said a lot of things," said Jake.

"You were arrested in a rogue Jaeger built from stolen tech, Jake."

"Wasn't mine."

"You have priors. This is serious," said Mako.

Jake's smile fell. "Which is why I need my big sister to get me the hell out of here."

"They're not going to let you just walk. But there might be another way . . ." said Mako.

"Great. Love it. What do I gotta do?" asked Jake.

"Reenlist. And finish what you started," said Mako.

Jake eyed Mako in surprise. Then, a laugh escaped him. "I'm a little old to be a cadet."

"I don't want you to be a cadet. I want you to help *train* them."

Jake glowered. "What's behind door number two?" he asked.

"The transport is standing by to bring both of you to Moyulan," said Mako.

"Both of us?"

"You and your new recruit." Mako smirked. "Enjoy your flight Jake!"

Mako's hologram winked off.

"Mako? Mako! Son of a . . . !" said Jake.

He knew he was trapped, and officially out of options.

03

The sunset cast a deep red shade over the Moyulan Shatterdome. Technicians hustled back and forth to refuel the Jumphawks, the aircrafts that deployed the Jaegers. A transport carrier landed on the tarmac. Jake and Amara walked out.

"Yeah, but why me? I mean why do they want me for the program?" asked Amara. She was hurrying to keep up with Jake's stride.

"Built and piloted your own Jaeger. Don't see that every day," said Jake.

At that moment, a shadow passed over them. Amara looked up at the sky. It was Scrapper being flown in via two Jumphawks! Amara beamed at the sight. The Jumphawks released Scrapper. The little Jaeger landed on her feet— then face-planted into the tarmac.

"Hey! Be careful with Scrapper!" shouted Amara.

"Will you look at this?"

Jake recognized the familiar voice.

He turned to face Nate. His friend still looked the same—military tank top, dog tags that jangled off his chest, and of course, a walk that made it seem like he owned the place.

"Didn't believe it when they told me you were inbound," said Nate.

"Nate. This is Cadet Amara Namani," said Jake.

"You'll address me as *Ranger* Lambert," said Nate.

"You having a laugh?" asked Jake.

"This is a military base," said Nate. "Remember how those work, Ranger Pentecost? Let's get you squared away." Nate started walking. Jake and Amara followed him through the base.

Amara leaned into Jake. "Did that haircut just call you Pentecost, as in badass Stacker Pentecost, pilot of Coyote Tango, hero of—"

"It's just a name," snapped Jake.

"A really cool name. Explains why you got a golden ticket."

"You know, moving forward, let's limit the conversation, okay?" Jake turned away from Amara. This wasn't a conversation he wanted to have with anyone, least of all this overly curious cadet. Nate pushed through the thirty-foot-tall ocean doors that led to Jaeger Bay. Jake felt a rush of wind hit his face. Amara's eyes widened in wonder.

This was the most amazing thing she had ever seen! Jaeger after Jaeger lined the shore. These were some of the most powerful machines in the world, and they were all in pristine condition! Nothing like the scraps and hunks of metal she was used to seeing in the yard back home.

"Sim training starts at 0600. You're late, you miss the day. Fall behind, you're on a transport back to wherever they found you," said Nate.

Amara barely heard him. "That's Titan Redeemer! And Bracer Phoenix, she's a three-man rig! And Guardian Bravo! And Saber Athena! I love Saber Athena! She's the fastest Jaeger in the fleet."

Jake nodded toward the techs running up and down the shore. "What's all the hustle for?"

"Been ordered to put on a show. Shao and her team arrive tomorrow," Nate explained.

"Shao? Like Shao Liwen?" asked Amara.

"What they tell me," said Nate.

Amara couldn't contain her excitement. Half the tech in Scrapper came from old Shao parts. "I can't believe I'm going to meet her!" she said aloud.

"You're not," said Nate.

"What? Why?"

"Why do you think. You're a cadet."

"That's not fair!"

"Get used to it around here," said Jake.

Amara huffed.

She turned to Nate. "So which one is yours?" she asked, motioning at the Jaegers.

Nate looked straight at Jake when he answered. "Gipsy."

"You pilot Gipsy Avenger?" asked Amara.

"He used to . . ." a bright voice chimed in from behind Amara. A woman outfitted in tech gear had driven up to them in a scrambler.

". . . until his copilot got a better offer in the private sector. I'm Jules Reyes," the woman shook Amara's hand.

"Amara. Cadet."

"Jake. Uh, Ranger, I guess."

Jules smiled. "Heard a lot about you, Pentecost. You know, you still hold the record."

Jake noticed Nate tighten at the comment.

"What record?" asked Amara.

"How'd they lure you back?" she asked. "Couldn't have been the pay."

"Long story," said Jake. "If you'd like to hear it sometime . . ." he swayed toward her.

"—She wouldn't," said Nate. "This what you were looking for?" he asked.

Nate handed Jules a machine part, and she smiled up at him. Jake noticed the way the two looked at each other. What was that about? And why did he suddenly care?

Canisters stacked near a scrambler fell down and crashed to the ground. The commotion distracted Jake from his thoughts. A tech barked harsh words at Hermann Gottlieb, a scientist for the Pan Pacific Defense Corps.

"The hell's the matter with you? Watch where you're going moron," said the tech.

Nate rushed to Gottlieb's side. "Yo, Gottlieb. You okay?" he asked.

"Oh, yes, sorry," said Gottlieb. He grinned and waved his burnt lab notes at Nate. "Almost had it." Then Gottlieb turned and headed out of the bay.

His head sunk down to review his notes.

"He's weird," said Amara.

"You have no idea," said Jules. "Welcome to the Moyulan Shatterdome, Cadet. Ranger." Then she drove off. Jake couldn't help but smile as he watched her go.

"Eyes front, Pentecost," said Nate.

"What record was she talking about?" asked Amara.

Jake tried to ignore the question but Amara didn't give up. "Come on, we were in jail together!" she urged.

"Part of the final exam, back when I was a cadet. You had to hold a drift in one of the old Mark IIIs for over twenty minutes."

"How long'd you last?"

"Little over four hours," said Jake.

Amara gaped. "Who was your copilot?"

Jake instinctively glanced at Nate, but Nate looked back at Amara. "Keep up, Cadet! Time to meet the rest of the family."

Amara walked into the cadet barracks. The room was full of teens like her—boys and girls from different places who had also ended up in this intense training program. The room was loud, rowdy, and full of life. Amara had the strange feeling, deep down inside of her, that she had finally made it home.

Two of the girls worked a holographic Jaeger arm with practice drift helmet rigs. The one named Meilin shouted, "You're outta sync," to the other girl, Vik, who muttered in Russian. "Ugh, this piece of junk—the helmet's acting up!" Vik threw off the helmet and shot Amara a dirty look.

Then two other cadets rushed past Amara, practicing martial arts. "Come on, not the face, Renata!" said Suresh. "Sorry, my bad," said Renata, who then smacked him in the chops again. Amara couldn't help but admire her lightning-fast combat skills. She would have to ask her for some pointers later! There was also a boy, named Jinhai, doing sit-ups off the edge of his upper bunk, while another kid named Ryoichi sat on his legs to help him keep balance. Two cadets named Ilya and Tahima played cards on the bunk beneath. The door behind Amara crashed open.

Nate entered with Jake. "Ranger on deck!" screamed Ryoichi. Jinhai backflipped off the top bunk and all the cadets scrambled into line formation.

"Cadets, this is Amara Namani," said Nate. "She'll be joining you in sim training, bright and early!" All the cadets in the bunk stared at Amara.

"And this is Ranger Pentecost."

A murmur spread through the room. The familiar sound of people recognizing his last name. Jake gritted his teeth. "He'll be helping me instruct you until I find a new copilot to replace Ranger Burke," said Nate. "Anything you want to add?" he asked Jake.

"Not really," Jake said. Nate glowered. If Jake wasn't going to at least pretend to help, then there was no point in him being here. He looked back at the cadets in the room. "Malikova, get Namani squared away and prepped for training."

"Yes, sir," said Vik.

"As you were," commanded Nate. He and Jake exited the room. Jake frowned at the cadets as he left. This was the last place in the world he thought he'd end up.

The room erupted as soon as the rangers were out of view. "Pentecost! We're gonna be trained by a Pentecost," exclaimed Ryoichi.

"So? It's not like he was the one who died helping close the Breach," said Vik. She looked back at the helmet in her hand and started taking it apart to troubleshoot it. Amara walked toward her. "Uh, hey, so where do I—"

Vik didn't look up. She just kept working on the helmet. "Heard you built your own little Jaeger," Vik said.

"Yeah, Scrapper. I operated her too with this solo rig that I—"

"You want to put junk together, be a mechanic. Moyulan is for *pilots*." Then she moved away. Amara felt like maybe her impulse about this place was wrong. Maybe it was just one more place she didn't belong. But then Jinhai approached her, a smile on his face. "Come on, I got you," he said. He took her duffel bag and led her through the barracks.

"Jinhai. Ou-Yang Jinhai," he said, giving Amara his full name.

"Ou-Yang? Like the pilots from the war, Ming-hau and Suyin?" Amara asked.

"I just call them mom and dad," he said. "So you and Vik already buddies, huh?"

"What's her problem?" asked Amara.

"Took her three shots to pass the entrance test," Renata chimed in.

"Don't think she likes how you landed here," said Jinhai.

"Not my fault," said Amara. "Recruiters never come around back home." Amara thought about the war-torn streets of Santa Monica with its junkyards and hungry people.

"Heard you were from the coast," said Jinhai. "Why didn't your folks move inland, like everyone else? They poor or something?"

"They didn't make it. When Santa Monica got hit."

Jinhai looked at Amara. He saw the pain behind her eyes. For someone so young, he could tell that she had experienced a lot of pain and loss. Not so different from any of the other cadets in the room.

"Vik lost hers, too, in the Tomari attack. Hey, know any Russian?" he asked.

Amara shook her head no.

"I'll teach you some. Calms her down. Let's stow your gear and get you a uniform." Amara followed him. She was grateful to have found a friend.

Jake stood in his room. He looked up at the ranger uniform that hung on the outside of his closet. It looked sharp, important, full of promise. He felt the material between his fingertips and thought about his past. He had spent so many years trying to put distance between himself and this world. Now he was back here, with Nate, because of Mako. Inside himself, he felt anger, regret, sorrow, and hope. He wondered where the uniform would lead him this time, and if he even deserved to wear it.

04

It was time to put their skills to the test. Amara and Suresh entered the training simulator in their cadet drivesuits. Once they were in their cradles, the two began to drift.

Amara and Suresh were suddenly in Titan Redeemer, and they were being attacked by the Category II Kaiju named Onibaba. Amara knew this was just training, but the simulator made the threat feel very real. The Kaiju lashed at Titan Redeemer. In response, Titan Redeemer deployed his morning star hand. But the Kaiju hit it aside and tore into the Jaeger. Amara and Suresh got slammed hard. Then the computer screamed: "Warning! Hemispheres out of alignment! Warning!"

"We need to reconnect!" said Suresh. "I'm trying!" screamed Amara.

BOOM! The conn-pod was hit again. This time, Amara and Suresh plunged into darkness.

A bright light flared and the conn-pod grinder opened.

Jake, Nate, and the rest of the cadets stood there. Everyone was looking at Amara.

"When I heard you gave November Ajax a run for his money, thought we might have something here. Now, not so much," said Nate.

Vik snickered in the background. Amara tore her helmet off. Her face was red with embarrassment and anger.

"How am I supposed to drift in this thing? It smells like feet!" she said.

"I ask you to open your mouth, Cadet?" Nate crossed his arms and stared at her.

Jake stepped forward and challenged Nate. "You're putting her up against a Kaiju that almost killed veteran pilots. She's not ready for that."

"Then maybe she's not the only one who doesn't belong here," Nate said to Jake.

"You got a problem with me, I'm right here. She's just a kid!"

"So were we!" screamed Nate. "That's the point. You make stronger connections when you're young. That kind of bond makes better pilots that can drift with anyone in their squad—"

"Yeah, I remember the pitch. Thanks." Jake shook his head. Then, he returned to his station.

Nate glowered. "Ryoichi, Renata, you're up. Show our new recruit how it's done."

Amara unhooked from the cradle.

The big industrial kitchen at the Shatterdome was empty late at night. Nate entered, stopping short. Somebody was rummaging in the freezer. He proceeded quietly until he got a clear view of Jake in his shorts, a rock T-shirt, flip-flops, and of course, a flashy bathrobe.

"Classy," said Nate.

Jake spun around to face Nate. He motioned at his outfit. "Jules loves it. Told me it's nice to finally have someone with style around here," he joked. Then he opened the refrigerator door, grabbed a beer, and tossed it to Nate.

Nate nodded his appreciation and cracked it open. "Chunky Monkey's in the bottom left, behind the frozen burgers."

Jake pulled out the big container of ice cream.

"Cheers," he said.

He continued to grab supplies from the cupboards to build a sundae. Lambert eyed him.

"So one more time around to prove daddy wrong?" asked Nate.

"Nah, just came back to see if your chin implant ever settled in." Jake smirked.

Nate couldn't help but laugh. "Looks good, doesn't it?"

Jake gave him a small smile back. "Very commanding. The kids must love it."

"They look up to us, man. We need to set an example. Show 'em how to work together."

Jake loudly sprayed whipped cream. "War ended ten years ago," he said.

"Gotta understand your enemy's objective to know you defeated them. We still don't," said Nate.

"I'm guessing it had something to do with sending giant monsters to kick the crap out of us," said Jake.

"The Precursors wouldn't send Kaiju to flatten a couple of cities if they were trying to wipe us all out. That's not a plan, genius."

"Look, I got no beef with you, Nate. I'm here because you and your squint was a better deal than some big hairy dude in a tiny little cell."

"I'm touched," said Nate.

"Cadets got what, a couple of months before they graduate?" asked Jake.

"Six," said Nate.

"*Six?*" said Jake. "Okay. Six. Tell you what. From now on, whenever you say something soldiery to them, I'll nod all like, yeah, what he said, and before you know it, they get to be pilots and I get to go back to my life."

"May happen sooner than you think," said Nate.

"How's that?" asked Jake.

"Big dog and pony show tomorrow. Shao Industries is pushing some kind of new drone tech. Could make all us pilots obsolete."

"Well that sounds like my get-out-of-jail-free card," said Jake.

Nate shook his head. "Front all you want Pentecost, but you know you could've been great if you had stuck around."

"I didn't bail. I was kicked out," said Jake.

"And whose fault was that?" asked Nate.

Nate tossed his beer can into the trash as he walked out of the room. His words dug into Jake.

The next morning, Nate and Jake followed Marshal Quan to Jaeger Bay. They slung on their bomber jackets as they stepped outside. It was a clear day and the water glistened in the distance.

Shao Liwen approached them. Everything Jake had heard about her was true. She looked sharp, meticulous, and intimidating. She was accompanied by her security chief, Kang, along with three of his men. Joseph Burke, the ex-military ranger who used to be Nate's partner, also strode confidently beside her.

Jake spotted Mako and Newt Geiszler trailing behind Shao and her team. Mako was in her PPDC uniform, and looked the same as ever. Newt, on the other hand, had been transformed completely by the private sector. This was no longer the half-crazy scientist who ran around in his lab coat dispensing random Kaiju facts. Now, Newt was wearing an expensive suit and his hair was slicked back.

Marshal stepped forward and greeted them: "Ms. Shao. Marshal Quan. It's an honor to meet you." Quan extended his hand, but Shao Liwen just eyed it uncomfortably.

Newt rushed to her side, not missing a beat. "Sorry, sorry, she doesn't do the whole hand thing," he explained, grabbing Quan's hand himself. "Dr. Newton Geiszler, head of research and devel—Whoa, that's a firm grip!" Newt turned to Shao, trying his best to repeat the phrase in Mandarin.

Shao looked at Marshal Quan and said in Mandarin, "Thank you for having us. Where can Mr. Burke and I set up?" The Marshal responded in perfect Mandarin, "Ranger Lambert and I will get you squared away, ma'am." Then he nodded to Mako and said, "We'll be in the war room, Madam Secretary."

"Thank you Marshal," she said.

Nate smiled at Mako. Then he reluctantly headed off with Quan, Liwen, and Burke. As Shao Liwen passed Jake, she gave him a long studied look.

Mako walked up to Jake. He grinned. He had always considered Mako to be his sister.

"Good to see you again," said Jake.

"That's a much better look on you," said Mako.

Newt jumped toward them. "Is this him? What am I talking about, of course it's him! Newton Geiszler, pleased to meet you. Gotta say, huge fan of your old man." Newt shook Jake's hand. "Today, we are canceling the apocalypse!" Newt said, mimicking Jake's dad. "Love that, use it all the time."

Jake was about to respond when suddenly Gottlieb appeared. He ran over to his old friend. "Ah! Newton! I was hoping you'd be tagging along. I could use your help on an experiment—"

Gottlieb rushed into the lab with Newt in tow. He hurriedly started setting things up.

"This will only take a moment. I don't want to impose, but—"

"Hey come on," Newt cut Gottlieb off. "We've been in each other's *heads*. Without the intel we yanked from that Kaiju brain, Raleigh never would have been able to close the Breach. That was you and me, pal." Then Newt checked his watch. "But I am running a little tight, so . . ."

"Yes, ummm . . . deployment!" said Gottlieb. He searched through his cluttered terminal desk.

"Deployment?" asked Newt.

"Of Jaegers," explained Gottlieb. "Deploying them into combat via Jumphawks takes too much time. The amount of damage a Kaiju can inflict before—Ah! Here!" He pulled a pile of singed notes off the desk and handed them to Newt. "I think I've found a solution."

Newt eyed Gottlieb's scribblings and then chuckled. "Rocket thrusters?" Newt asked. "There's no fuel in the world with that kind of boost-to-mass ratio."

"From *this* world, no," said Gottlieb. He presented Newt with a vial of neon blue liquid. Newt tensed.

"Kaiju blood?" asked Newt.

"Exactly!" said Gottlieb excitedly. "I've discovered it's highly reactive when combined with rare earth elements like cerium, lanthanum, gadolinium . . ."

"Dude, you can't be fooling around with this stuff! You're going to blow yourself up," said Newt. Then he held up the singed lab notes. "Look at these! You already did, didn't you? You done went and blew yourself up."

"I just need to balance the equation. No one knows more about Kaiju morphology than you, Newt. If you could just take a look—"

"Buddy, it doesn't matter. Once my boss's drones are approved, deployment time'll be a nonissue. Within a year we'll have drones everywhere."

"So you won't help me?" Gottlieb asked.

Newt's watch beeped. He frowned an apology and started to leave. "Sorry. Duty calls. Been nice catching up."

"Newton?" said Gottlieb. "I—I still have nightmares. About what we saw. When we drifted with that disgusting Kaiju brain."

"Yeah. But sure was a hell of a rush, wasn't it?" asked Newt in a soft voice.

"No one knows what it felt like. To be in its mind. Except *us*. You and I. *Together*," replied Gottlieb.

Newt heard the pleading in Gottlieb's voice for help, for friendship. He struggled with how to answer it. He wanted to respond, but just as he was about to say the words, he was interrupted by Shao's security chief, Kang.

"Dr. Geiszler. Time to go," Kang said firmly.

"Okay, okay," said Newt. He mustered a smile at Gottlieb and then followed the chief away. Gottlieb watched him go, feeling completely and utterly alone.

Shao strode quickly down the long corridor. Newt hustled to keep pace with his boss. Kang and his men trailed behind them, but Shao was focused on Newt.

"You and Dr. Gottlieb were close, weren't you? During the war," she said.

"Hermann? We shared lab yes okay," said Newt in broken Mandarin.

"*English*. Your Mandarin makes you sound like an idiot," said Shao.

"Um, yes. We shared a lab," said Newt in English.

"He was your friend?" asked Shao.

Newt hesitated. The word reminded him of the past. He had been close to Gottlieb during the war. Not only had they accomplished a lot together, he did see him as a friend. One of the closest people to him during that time, to be sure.

"Yeah. He was," said Newt finally.

"What were you and Dr. Gottlieb talking about?" Shao asked.

"Nothing. Just some nutty idea he has about thruster pods," said Newt.

"I can't afford a misstep before Secretary-General Mori makes her recommendation at the council summit.

No more contact with Dr. Gottlieb until after the vote," said Shao.

"But he's harmless—" said Newt.

Shao snapped at him angrily, in fast Mandarin.

"Uh, could you say that again? About 80 percent slower?" asked Newt.

"I said don't make me question your loyalty."

"No, no question. We barely talk anyway."

"Then it won't be a problem," said Shao. "And work on your Mandarin. I don't like to repeat myself, in any language."

Shao marched out of the room. Newt followed, his emotions as complicated and mixed up as ever.

Inside the war room at the Moyulan Shatterdome, a massive hologram displayed a drone Jaeger in all its glory. Liwen addressed the ranger Jaeger pilots and J-Techs, including Jules. Newt beamed at his boss while Burke, Jake, Nate, Mako, Gottlieb, and Quan looked on.

"The system I designed processes commands through a quantum data core, relieving the neural load. This means that a single pilot can operate the drone via remote link from anywhere in the world. As soon as the council approves deployment, the days of struggling to find and train drift-compatible pilots will be a thing of the past," explained Shao.

Dissatisfied murmurs rumbled through the room. The rangers were especially riled. Gottlieb wiped his glasses and squinted at the drone in scientific curiosity.

"You think a bunch of desk jockeys playing with their joysticks can stop a Kaiju attack?" asked Nate.

"Not only can they stop it, they can do so without putting pilots at unnecessary risk, Nate," said Burke.

Shao nodded. "Contrary to what you may have heard, we're not here to shut you down."

"Cooperation between our programs has never been more vital. If there are any questions . . ." said Burke.

The room exploded in a cacophony of questions from the pilots and techs. They were not buying what Shao was selling. Neither was Jake. A frown settled on his face as he exited the room. Mako followed him.

"That was pretty slick. How long before they shut all this down and I can go home?" spat Jake.

"I don't trust the tech. Not yet, at least," said Mako. She followed him out onto a catwalk overlooking Jaeger Bay. Gipsy Avenger loomed in the distance.

"Looked dialed in to me," said Jake.

"Remote systems can be hacked or compromised," said Mako.

"Well you're the key vote, right? Your decision, so there you go," said Jake.

Mako stared into the distance. "I wish I could just go ahead and approve them. If we had drones back in the war, maybe dad would still be alive."

Her eyes settled on Gipsy. "And Raleigh."

"What'd that have to do with the war? News said it was cancer," said Jake, confused.

"Everything about the other side of the Breach is still classified. There's a kind of radiation, in the Anteverse. We didn't know how bad it was until it was too late."

Jake tensed. "Are you all right?"

Mako nodded, but the memory was painful for her. "Raleigh ejected me. I got sick and couldn't pilot anymore, but I'm okay now. He got the worst of it."

Jake absorbed that. "I'm sorry. I didn't know," he said.

"We can't change the past. But the future is ours to make," said Mako.

A weight pressed down on her. "A lot of people want to see the drones deployed. Nearly half the council is backing Liwen. They aren't going to like my decision," said Mako.

"How about I go with you for some moral support? Never been to Sydney, hear it's great," said Jake.

Mako brightened. "I'm glad you offered, because I've already requested Gipsy Avenger for honor guard at the council summit."

"Whoa, hold up. Honor guard?" said Jake. "That's not what I meant."

"What about my moral support?" said Mako, playfully.

"Gipsy is Nate's ride," said Jake.

Mako grinned. "His copilot works for Liwen now. He needs a new one . . ."

"One that you already know is drift compatible, right," said Jake. He laughed. "I see what you're trying to do, putting me back in a live rig."

Mako smiled. "I have no idea what you're talking about."

Jake thought about it for a minute. Then he smiled back.

"Alright, sis. I got your back."

Jake thought for a minute more, and his smile grew. "But I want to be there when you tell him. He's gonna be so pissed, he'll make that face like—"

Jake made a funny, rigid face—a perfect impression of his friend.

Mako laughed. Then she looked to the side, and her face dropped. Something was weighing on her . . .

05

The PPDC council building loomed over the city of Sydney. Massive anti-Kaiju cannons lined the coastline. The streets were pristine and clean, with sharp glass and metal buildings rising in the air. Unlike most of the coastal slums, Sydney was heavily protected. No safety measure had been spared when it came to protecting the PPDC headquarters.

The streets swirled with people. PPDC security desperately tried to keep the massive crowd in check as dignitaries from around the world arrived for the summit council hearing.

In the middle of the crowd, red nuns stood solemnly together. They were a part of the Kaiju worshippers, people who believed that the Kaiju were sacred beings. From the depths of their gathering, a man shouted, "Kaiju were sent by God to purge us of our sins! To resist them is to turn from the Almighty—"

A scuffle broke out as an angry man wearing a Jaeger

T-shirt tried to grab the sign away from the worshipper. Then, suddenly, a shadow appeared over the sky.

Gipsy Avenger was being flown in via Jumphawks. The crowd of people grew silent as they watched the glistening metal Jaeger glide above them.

Inside the Moyulan Shatterdome, Marshal Quan strode over to a woman named Xiang who was working the holo screen for the Jaeger.

"How are they doing?" he asked.

"Hemispheres are calibrated. Neural handshake is weak but holding," Xiang answered.

"Gipsy Avenger, this is Marshal Quan," he said, initiating communication between home base and the Jaeger.

Jake and Nate stood in their drift cradles. Jake fidgeted. His heart hadn't stopped racing since he got into this thing. Directly across from him, Nate scowled. He was clearly unhappy with the pairing.

"All you have to do is stand there and look pretty. Stay focused and try not to fall over," said the marshal.

"Roger that, sir," said Nate.

"Go for drop in three, two, one . . . drop!"

Gipsy Avenger released from the Jumphawks.

KA-THOOM! A shockwave of dust surged across the crowd as she landed. The Jaeger nearly lost her footing.

Jake steadied himself. Nate shot him a frown.

"It's all coming back. Relax," Jake said. Then he frowned at the protestors on Gipsy's display. A worshipper threw a bottle at Gipsy. The PPDC security started making arrests. "Got some fans, huh?"

"Kaiju nuts are always stirring it up," said Nate. "And hey—we're in each other's heads, so I'd appreciate it if you'd stop thinking about Jules. Not gonna happen."

"How about you stop thinking about beating me up. Not gonna happen either."

Nate tightened. An incoming chopper pinged on the display. A readout listed the only passenger: Mako Mori, Secretary-General, PPDC Security Council.

Inside the chopper, Mako absentmindedly sketched a strange Kaiju head on her data pad. She spotted Gipsy Avenger in the distance through the window. A smile appeared on her lips, tinged with mysterious relief.

Shao's limo approached the council building. She climbed out of the car, surrounded by Kang and his men. Suddenly, a loud sound like a tanker ship venting ballast turned her and the crowd around. A huge spray of water erupted in the harbor! Shao looked to find its source, but buildings blocked her view.

Inside Gipsy Avenger, some huge foreign object pinged on the display. "Gipsy to Command, you reading this?" Nate said.

Xiang looked at the holo screen inside the Moyulan Shatterdome and tensed. "It's a Jaeger sir, but it's not broadcasting a CSD," she said to Marshal Quan.

"Gipsy, this is Command," said Quan over the speaker. "Be advised we have an unregistered Jaeger, no call sign designation."

The unregistered Jaeger exploded out of the bay and landed like a panther on the street. Inside her helicopter, Mako constricted at the sight of the machine. Nate and Jake also tensed as the sleek and advanced machine moved eerily quickly through the streets of Sydney.

Jake eyed the holo display, scanning the mysterious Jaeger. "What is that? Is that one of ours?"

"Pilots of unregistered Jaeger, power down and exit your conn-pod immediately," ordered Nate over the loudspeaker. "I repeat: Power down and exit your conn-pod immediately—"

The unregistered Jaeger responded to Nate's plea by unleashing a barrage of plasma missiles into the air!

Xiang's plasma screen lit up and tracked the missiles. The room around her exploded with noise as her team tried to figure out what was going on. "Missiles fired! Multiple ordnance inbound," screamed Marshal Quan. The missiles struck the anti-Kaiju cannons, and a few slammed into Gipsy Avenger and the council building. They were definitely under attack by this rogue Jaeger. Its name was Obsidian Fury.

Warning alarms wailed. "Neural handshake fluctuating," said Xiang, as she watched Gipsy Avenger's activity on her screen.

Inside, Jake struggled to maintain control of the Jaeger. This was his first time in actual combat—not a simulator, no second chances. Time slowed. His breath filled his ears. A voice reached out to him from long ago. It was the voice of his father.

"You don't belong in a Jaeger!" the voice echoed in Jake's ears, distorted and distant.

"Jake! Stay connected! Jake!" shouted Nate. But then suddenly, WHOOSH! Both of them were sucked into Jake's memory.

Alarms wailed as another volley of plasma missiles slammed into Gipsy. Nate shook himself out of the drift memory.

"Jake! *Pentecost*!" screamed Nate.

Jake snapped out of the memory. He was rattled and disoriented. "What . . . what do we do?" he asked.

"Stay focused. Follow my lead, and look out—"

A chunk of the council building crashed down, falling quickly toward the crowd below. Nate shot out his hand and Gipsy Avenger caught the chunk a second before it hit the crowd of people. Kang and his men rushed Shao toward her limo as more plasma missiles soared through the air, slamming into Gipsy Avenger.

Mako tensed. Her data pad picked up an odd power signal from Obsidian. "Jake! That Jaeger's power is reading the same as—"

A piercing screech suddenly split the air. Obsidian Fury was jamming the comms!

A warning alarm wailed as they got rocked with another blast. The lights flickered. Jake eyed a flashing holo screen. "We're losing power!" he warned.

"Rerouting systems," said Nate, as his fingers flew across the holo screen.

Jake saw Obsidian Fury raise a particle cannon—aiming it directly at Mako's helicopter.

"Nate!" screamed Jake. He needed him to rush.

"Power's up!" Nate yelled.

Jake hurled a chunk of building at the evil Jaeger. Debris rained down on the city, only barely missing Shao and the rest of the fleeing crowd. The building chunk made contact and Obsidian Fury went flying backwards.

Then Gipsy Avenger slammed into Obsidian Fury with all its weight. Obsidian responded by tearing at Gipsy with vicious metal claws. Gipsy staggered back into a building. It almost trampled a crowd of people as Jake and Nate struggled to steady Gipsy.

Obsidian seized the distraction, grabbed Gipsy by the leg, and slammed her into a row of buildings. It started to rip at Gipsy's head.

Nate desperately punched commands on a holo pad that sprung up from his drivesuit's forearm. Gipsy Avenger's chain sword shot out. It forced Obsidian to let go. Then Gipsy swung, but Obsidian kicked Gipsy into a building. The evil Jaeger flexed both arms, and twin plasma chain saws sprung from them!

Obsidian Fury and Gipsy Avenger clashed in battle. Office workers scrambled out of the way as the chain saws tore through a building,

"Are those chain saws? Does that thing have chain saws?" asked Jake.

Gipsy Avenger slammed into Obsidian Fury again. Arcs of energy rippled into the air as the two machines clashed.

"We need to land!" the pilot of the helicopter shouted at Mako.

"No! We have to help them! Target that Jaeger!" commanded Mako.

The pilot complied with a grimace. "Target locked!"

"Fire!" said Mako.

The pilot jammed the fire button on his stick. Mako's helicopter unleashed a barrage of missiles. They hit the evil Jaeger's arm, causing it to miss Gipsy and nearly splitting an office building down the middle with its chain saw. Office workers scrambled out of the way as the plasma chain saw tore through the building.

The chain saw momentarily got stuck! Gipsy Avenger took advantage of the moment and hit Obsidian Fury with a supersonic punch. The rogue Jaeger flew back, but it used its chain saws to gouge into the buildings, creating enough friction to help it slow down. Then it fired another round of deadly plasma missiles into the air!

The missiles peppered the city. One hit a parking garage, and the cars inside smashed down on the people below. Another detonated close to Mako Mori, and the explosion forced her helicopter to begin to drop out of the sky.

"She's going down! We need to move!" screamed Jake.

"Activating gravity sling!" replied Nate.

Gipsy Avenger's right arm formed into the gravity sling weapon, which could use gravitational forces to lift objects and then fire them at a target. A wave of distortion flew out of Gipsy's rotating blue arm. It scooped up falling cars from the parking garage and launched them at Obsidian Fury. The cars hit and Obsidian Fury flew backwards through the air. Gipsy Avenger turned and raced across the city to save Mako's copter.

Mako watched as Gipsy raced toward her. She desperately tried to send a message from her data pad.

Jake struggled against his drift cradle, pushing Gipsy Avenger to her limits. Nate did the same. As Mako's helicopter plummeted, Gipsy leaped into the air and reached out to catch it. And missed.

Mako put her hand to the window as the helicopter dropped and then crashed into the ground. The helicopter skidded across the asphalt and smashed cars as it careened down the street. Gipsy crashed to the ground from its missed leap, and the windows of the surrounding buildings exploded from the force.

Jake dropped down from a hatch on Gipsy Avenger's head and ran full tilt toward Mako. His face was full of horror and fear. He ripped off his helmet as he sprinted to reach the smoking wreckage of the destroyed copter.

Obsidian Fury started to move toward a downed Gipsy Avenger, but then three other PPDC Jaegers flew into Sydney via Jumphawks. So instead, Obsidian Fury turned away and slunk back into the water. Its metal disappeared beneath the waves.

06

Jake stood in the Hall of Heroes. In front of him, a plaque read: IN HONOR OF THOSE WHO GAVE THEIR LIVES IN THE SERVICE OF THEIR WORLD.

Digital memorial screens lined the wall.

Raleigh Becket. Copilot of Gipsy Danger who, with Mako Mori, saved the world by crossing the Breach and entering the Anteverse.

Yancy Becket. Raleigh's brother and original copilot of Gipsy Danger. After completing many successful missions in the Kaiju Wars, Yancy gave his life in a battle off the coast of Anchorage in an attempt to save a fishing vessel.

Chuck Hansen. Copilot of Striker Eureka during the Kaiju Wars. He died in the Battle of the Breach alongside Stacker Pentecost. They sacrificed themselves so that Raleigh and Mako could cross the Breach—a heroic sacrifice still honored and celebrated around the world.

The Wei Tang triplets. The pilots of Crimson Typhoon during the Kaiju Wars. They killed seven Kaiju, before losing their lives in battle.

Sasha and Aleksis Kaidanovsky. The husband and wife pilot Jaeger team that hailed from Russia. They killed six Kaiju before also losing their lives in battle.

Jake stood in front of a memorial—Stacker Pentecost. His father was in full uniform. His stern face looked down at Jake.

Slightly to the right was a brand new memorial for Mako. She was also in full uniform, and her face beamed with pride for the Jaeger pilot program. Spread around Mako's memorial were fresh flowers and candles, placed there by mourners. Jake stepped up to her memorial.

"I'll hit 'em back for you, Mako," he said. Then he taped up a photograph of their family—Stacker with his arms around a young Mako and a young Jake.

Suddenly, a noise pulled his attention to a door labeled DRIFT TRAINING—CADET LEVEL I. Muffled yelling came from inside. He entered the room.

"Neural connection failed," said a computer voice.

Amara punched a holo screen, getting madder and madder. Then, she saw Jake. It was the first time she had seen him since the Sydney attack. She tried to find the right words but couldn't.

"Hey," she said.

"Hey," said Jake.

"So I'm not great with feelings, but I'm sorry about your sister. Half sister?" she said uncertainly.

"Her parents died in the Onibaba attack. My dad took her in. She was *my sister. My family.*"

The weight of the loss crushed down on Jake. Amara was still unsure of what to do. She tried to shift his focus.

"Better not let Ranger Lambert see you out of uniform. He'll take the stick out of his butt and beat you with it."

Her approach worked. Jake laughed. "Think I'm safe. It's wedged in there pretty tight."

He approached the drift rig Amara was punching. He saw that one side was occupied by a human brain floating in a container of synthetic cerebral fluid. A plaque mounted below the brain read: THIS IS SARAH. SHE DONATED HER MIND SO THAT YOU COULD TRAIN. TELL ME HER FAVORITE CANDY BAR.

Jake smiled. "They're still using Sarah, huh?"

"I can't get her to drift with me," said Amara. "The

other cadets have been training forever. Hate feeling like the slow kid."

"You gotta *relax*, or you're just grinding gears," said Jake

Jake punched holo commands. Sarah retracted. She was replaced by a regular drift rig.

"Relax. Got it, coach," said Amara.

"Don't call me coach," said Jake.

"Sensei?" joked Amara.

Jake took the drift helmet and slid it on. "Just shut up and clear your mind. Can't connect if you're running your mouth. You ready?"

Amara gave him the double thumbs up.

"Let's see if we're drift compatible . . ." said Jake.

Jake punched commands. Amara gasped as she got sucked into the drift space. Their minds were melding. Abstract memories rushed past.

Amara as a kid: laughing as she chased her brother through the backyard, her on a bicycle. Then her father teaching her how to rebuild a car engine in the garage.

The memories transitioned easily to Jake as a young boy in his father's study. He put on his dad's hat, which was way too big for him, and saluted. Young Jake in military school jogging in formation with a teenage Nate. Then, a younger Mako teaching Jake how to staff fight.

Then, they were sucked out of the drift. "Warning! Neural connection unstable," said a computer voice.

Jake whipped his eyes to a holo drift connection meter. The strength of their connection dropped down to the red zone.

"Stay focused," instructed Jake. Amara concentrated. The connection meter started to climb.

"That's it. The stronger the connection, the better you fight," said Jake.

Amara grinned. She was getting the hang of it. She picked up one of Jake's memories. "You lived in a mansion?" she joked, referring to the time he spent in an abandoned one in Santa Monica.

WHAM! Amara winced as a memory slammed into her.

The Santa Monica Pier. People running and screaming. She was little and standing frozen in the middle of the chaos, clutching a Polaroid photograph.

Jake winced. Warning alarms wailed. "Don't let a memory pull you in. Let them pass through you. Amara!"

Amara turned to Jake, but she didn't see him. Instead she was looking at—

Her father on the pier. Holding a Polaroid camera. "Amara! Get in there!" he screamed. She rushed past to join her mother and her big brother.

Jake was now standing on the pier as well, sucked into Amara's memory.

The family laughed. Click. Photo taken. Amara grabbed the Polaroid from her dad and ran to the railing, shaking the picture to accelerate development.

"Amara! You need to let it go—" said Jake.

Whoosh! A Kaiju burst out of the water behind young Amara. It took out a section of the pier. Young Amara was trapped on the ocean side of the pier, frozen in the chaos of the fleeing crowd. Her family was on the other side.

Amara spasmed. She was lost in the horror of the memory. "Warning. Pilot exceeding neural limits," said a computer voice.

Jake gritted his teeth and shouted to her. "Amara!"

Amara's father was motioning at her. "You have to jump!" he screamed. Young Amara hesitated—terrified. "Please baby, jump to me! I'll catch you, I promise! Amara!" screamed her dad. Amara ran and leapt into the air. Her father reached out and KA-THOOM! A Kaiju foot slammed down, obliterating her family. Young Amara hit the water. The shadow of the Kaiju passed overhead. She started to sink . . .

Jake's hand grabbed Amara, yanking her out of the memory. Amara was shaken. Almost nonresponsive. "Amara! Come on! Hey!" said Jake.

Amara snapped out of it. She looked around in a state of panic. She locked eyes with Jake. "I was back home. I felt it . . ." she explained.

Jake felt the weight of what happened to her in the past almost as keenly as if it had happened to him. "I felt it too," he said.

Jake's comm crackled to life, interrupting the moment. "Jake, it's Nate. You there?"

"Yeah, I'm here," said Jake.

"Meet me in the lab right away. Marshal wants to see us. And lose the robe," said Nate.

"Check. No robe," said Jake. He grinned at Amara.

A jumble of fragmented data swirled across a holographic screen in Gottlieb's lab. Jake and Nate stood with Marshal Quan.

"What is it?" asked Jake.

"A message. From Mako," said Marshal Quan.

The news hit Jake hard. He stared at the holographic data.

"She was trying to send it from her copter right before she—" Gottlieb caught himself. "It's a data packet, high density," he finished.

Nate looked confused. "Obsidian Fury was jamming comms. How'd her signal get through?"

"It didn't. At least not intact," Marshal Quan answered.

"So it's gone," said Jake.

At this, Gottlieb chirped up. "'Gone is relative in the digital realm. By running a modified fractal algorithm, I might be able to reconstruct a few megabytes . . ." Gottlieb tapped a few keys. "*There!*" he said.

A static-filled image of the strange Kaiju head that Mako had been drawing just before her copter went down appeared on the holo screen.

"Is that . . . is that a Kaiju?" asked Jake.

Gottlieb was working the terminal. "No match against the database," he said.

"Keep looking. Whatever this is, it was important to

her. I want to know why," said Marshal Quan. Then, he exited the room.

Nate stared at Mako's drawing. "You don't stop fighting till the enemy's down . . ." He looked up at Jake. ". . . If you're really a soldier." Then Nate followed Marshal Quan out.

Jake was left alone in the lab with Mako's drawing. He stared at the holo screen trying to make sense of it.

07

Newt walked through Shao Industries at night. His lab here was top-of-the-line—a high-tech marvel by anyone's standards. Lab techs in their twenties and thirties were busily working at their computer stations. Newt rushed in hurriedly and hissed at the tech next to him, "How long's *she* been here?" He pointed at Shao.

"Almost an hour," said the tech, named Daiyu.

Newt cursed under his breath as he crossed over to greet Shao. Her hands were buried deep in the guts of a drone Jaeger data core.

Burke stood next to her in a sharp-looking drone Jaeger telemetry suit. Cables ran from his VR helmet into the data core. Newt forced a smile.

"Hey boss. Sorry, thought you were still in Sydney," he said to Shao.

"The council has approved drone deployment in an emergency session," she replied.

"Wow, that's . . . that's great," Newt stammered.

"Thought you'd be a little more enthusiastic, Doc," said Burke.

"No, I am, it's just, you know. They're approving now because of the attack," said Newt.

"I was *there*. I know what happened," said Shao in English. Then she switched to Mandarin and said, "And it wouldn't have happened, if our drones had been in the field. Now *everyone* sees that."

"Yeah. I guess they do," said Newt.

"Which means the attack was positive. All things considered," said Shao in Mandarin again.

"If you look at it sideways and squint, then yeah I guess—" said Newt.

Shao disconnected Burke from the data core. "There's a 0.5-second micro delay in the uplink to the data cores," she said.

"I know. I'm working on boosting the connection," said Newt.

"Any other irregularities I should know about?" asked Shao.

"No. All systems double thumbs," answered Newt.

"Push your data to my server. I want to run a diagnostic.

The council expects full deployment in 48 hours." Shao switched back to English. "Get it done," she said firmly.

Shao swept out of the lab with Burke at her side.

Newt called after her. "Sure! No problem! I'm on it like a guy—like a guy that's really, really on it."

"What? No way we'll be ready!" whispered Daiyu in a harsh tone.

"Way? Way? Yes, way. Know what—you're fired. No, get this done, *then* you're fired. Or promoted. We'll see how it goes. But probably fired. Go! Shoo!" Newt exclaimed.

The techs peeled off as Newt walked up to an observation window. The window overlooked a massive automated factory where the drone Jaegers at Shao Industries were being fitted with data cores. Newt eyed them. He was worried about the schedule, despite his promises to Shao. He never could catch a break, he thought to himself.

Amara sat on her bunk bed, streaming the newsfeed of the Sydney attack. She studied the evil Jaeger's every move. Tahima peeked over Amara's shoulder and grunted in contempt.

"'Obsidian Fury.' Doesn't even sound like a real Jaeger name," said Tahima, motioning at the evil Jaeger.

"I don't think *Tahima* sounds like a real name, but your mama did," joked Renata.

"There's never been a rogue like this," said Amara. "How'd the Kaiju nuts build it? Ones where I'm from couldn't change a battery without getting fried."

"Maybe they stole it," said Ryoichi.

"Da. You can steal anything in my country with overalls and a work order," said Ilya.

Amara hadn't stopped looking at the feed. "These pilots . . . they're *too* fast. I don't understand how they're exceeding the neural load—"

"Ballerinas, I'm telling you," chimed in Jinhai.

"Stop it with that, man. You know how many people died in Sydney?" said Tahima.

"Newsfeed said they're posting a dozen Jaegers at the memorial," said Meilin.

"When I die, I want that many to send *me* off," said Suresh.

"Still you die—meh. I'd post *one* Jaeger at your funeral. Maybe *half* a Jaeger," said Jinhai.

"I heard that's where they found Amara. In half a Jaeger," said Vik, looking at Amara coldly.

Amara shot up. "It was a *whole* Jaeger. It just wasn't very big, *Viktoriya*."

Renata's mouth hung open after Amara used Vik's full name. This was getting good!

Vik stepped close to Amara, looming over her. "Bigger is better," she said.

Amara sized Vik up. She was much bigger. "Look, uh—*Idi na fig*," said Amara in Russian. Vik laughed in disbelief. Ilya, who was also Russian, tensed.

"What did you say?" said Vik.

"*Idi na . . . fig?*" Amara said hesitantly. "Am I saying that right?" she asked Jinhai.

"Yep," said Jinhai. He suppressed a laugh. The Russian phrase he taught Amara was obviously not a friendly one. Vik exploded and grabbed Amara in a chokehold.

"Whoa!" said Jinhai.

"Vik, come on! Let her go—" said Ryoichi.

"I worked every day of my life to be here! You didn't do anything! You were just picked up off the street like garbage!" Vik screamed.

Amara snapped. She broke free and took Vik down with a scissor lock around the neck. The cadets erupted in surprise as Vik struggled for air.

"Know where I learned that? On the *streets*, you big dumb—"

"Namani! Malikova!" screamed a voice. The cadets whirled around to face Nate.

"Ranger Lambert on deck," warned Ryoichi.

The cadets all stood at attention. Amara released Vik, and they both scrambled up.

"She jumped me—" said Amara.

"She does not belong here," said Vik.

"Enough!" screamed Nate. There was anger in his voice, but the cadets could also see the pain and loss in his eyes. Amara and Vik fell silent.

"When I first joined the corps, I was just like you. Worse even. I was nobody. From nowhere. But Mako Mori told me I could make a difference," said Nate.

Jake drifted into the room. He had heard Nate's words from outside the door, and they drew him in. He was still wearing his street clothes.

Nate continued. "She said whoever you are, wherever

you come from, the minute you enter this program, you're part of a family. And the people beside you are your brothers and sisters."

Nate cocked his head toward Jake. This speech was half meant for him.

"No matter what they do . . . no matter how stupid they act . . . you forgive. And you move on. Because that's what family does. Start believing that out here and you'll start believing it in a Jaeger."

Nate's words hit the room hard. Amara and Vik exchanged sheepish glances. Jake looked at Nate, suddenly understanding the hurt he caused his "brother" when he ran off years ago. Then, Jules entered the cadets' barracks.

"Hey," she said. Nate and Jake turned to face her. "Marshal's looking for you guys. Said Gottlieb found something."

The rangers rushed over to the lab. Gottlieb worked a holo screen, displaying Mako's Kaiju head drawing. It overlaid a section of topography. Jake, Nate, and Marshal Quan couldn't believe what they were seeing. Mako's drawing wasn't a Kaiju head. It was a map!

"Severnaya Zemlya. Off Siberia's Taymyr Peninsula," explained Gottlieb.

"What's in Zemlya?" asked Marshal Quan.

"Nothing anymore," said Gottlieb. He zoomed in on the eye of the drawing. "A facility roughly in this location was used to manufacture Jaeger power cores early in the war. But it was decommissioned years ago."

"Why would Mako be trying to tell us about an abandoned factory in the middle of nowhere?" asked Nate. Then he eyed Jake, challenging him.

Jake understood. He turned to Marshal Quan.

"Sir, permission to take Gipsy Avenger and see what's out there."

A howling swirl of ice and snow assaulted the frozen landscape. Gipsy Avenger blasted through the snow. The Jaeger paused, looking up at something in the distance.

It was a manufacturing facility built into the side of a glacier, the one Gottlieb had mentioned in the lab. A cascade of ice half sealed the abandoned and dilapidated structure.

Nate eyed the tactical scans of the facility on Gipsy's display.

"No life signs. Looks like Gottlieb was right. Place is abandoned," said Nate.

Then, the scan partially locked onto something deep inside the facility. It was faint and fluctuating.

"Wait a second. I'm picking up some weird readings—" said Jake.

WHOOM! Plasma missiles roared past Gipsy Avenger and destroyed the facility, obliterating any evidence that it might have contained. Gipsy whirled around to face Obsidian Fury, emerging out of a swirl of ice and snow!

Obsidian Fury loomed on Gipsy's screen. Jake snarled and hurled forward in his drift cradle. He was no longer afraid of Obsidian Fury. Now he just wanted revenge for Mako's death!

Gipsy charged at Obsidian. Obsidian unleashed another barrage of missiles. They slammed into Gipsy, but Gipsy ignored them and charged forward. "Get him off his feet," screamed Nate. Jake bellowed and leapt into the air.

WHAM! Gipsy Avenger tackled Obsidian Fury. Both Jaegers skidded across the ice and tumbled into a crevasse.

As she fell through the deep fracture in the ice, Gipsy unleashed her chain sword. Obsidian countered by revving up his chain saws. The Jaegers traded blows, bounced off an embankment, and—

—crashed through the ice wall and out onto an ice floe!

Obsidian was the first Jaeger to regain balance. He whirled to face Gipsy, and then fired a sustained blast from his chest disrupter. Gipsy hipped her chain sword up. The disruptor beam slammed into it, throwing off ribbons of energy.

Jake and Nate struggled to block the particle beam assault with their chain sword.

"We gotta get out of here!" said Nate.

Jake thought fast. He reared up his fist and slammed it down! Gipsy imitated the motion—her fist slam cracked the ice at her feet. Gipsy tumbled into the water. Jake and Nate braced as the ice gave way under them.

Obsidian Fury walked to the edge of the hole in the ice that Gipsy had just created and looked down. FHOOM! FHOOM! FHOOM! Detonations bloomed deep below in the water.

WHOOSH! Missiles exploded out of the hole. They arced up and crashed down all around Obsidian, blowing out the ice under the metal beast's feet. Obsidian Fury crashed into the water and started to sink.

Gipsy Avenger rushed up from the depths, propelled by maneuvering jets in her legs. She slammed into Obsidian Fury, driving the evil Jaeger up through the ice.

Gipsy and Obsidian Fury surged up through the ice, trading thunderous blows as they grappled. Obsidian started to get the upper hand, but then Gipsy blasted the Jaeger. Obsidian flew back and Gipsy rose to her feet.

"I think we pissed him off," said Nate.

"*Good*," said Jake.

Jake and Nate deployed Gipsy's chain sword.

Obsidian reacted by deploying his chain saws, but this time they turned into whirling blades. Jake and Nate exchanged a worried look. The two Jaegers charged at each other.

"Follow my lead!" said Jake.

Obsidian swung his blades to cut Gipsy's head off, but Gipsy ducked under the blow and sliced open Obsidian's chest.

"He's hurt!" said Jake.

"Go for his power core!" said Nate.

Jake stabbed out to destroy Obsidian's exposed power core, but Obsidian dodged the attack. Instead, Gipsy's sword sunk into Obsidian's thigh. Obsidian chopped off Gipsy's chain sword, sending Gipsy tumbling.

Obsidian Fury went in for the kill with his chain saws, but Gipsy caught the Jaeger's wrists. Obsidian Fury pressed, its saws gouging into Gipsy's head. The conn-pod was about to come apart! Nate and Jake strained with all their might to repel the attack.

Slowly, painfully, heroically, Gipsy Avenger forced the plasma chain saws away from her head and back into Obsidian's own chest. Obsidian reeled and Gipsy Avenger pressed the advantage—raining blows down on Obsidian. Jake and Nate gave the other Jaeger a beating!

Obsidian tried to counter with its chain saw. Gipsy dodged the blow and ripped the broken chain sword from Obsidian's leg, burying it in the Jaeger's neck.

Jake and Nate completed the stab to the neck and went in for the kill: Gipsy Avenger punched through Obsidian Fury's chest and ripped out its power core! The resulting energy surge fried Obsidian! The rogue Jaeger crumbled to the ground.

Jake surged forward. It was time to meet the pilots who had caused him so much pain.

Gipsy roughly grabbed Obsidian Fury and ripped the Jaeger's face off. Then Nate and Jake's expressions changed to horror. Inside Obsidian Fury's conn-pod, there were no Kaiju worshippers. No pilots at all!

Instead, it was a mass of Kaiju brain tissue with nerve tendrils that webbed out into the conn-pod's electronics! The brain, which was damaged in the energy surge, convulsed and died.

Jake felt robbed of his vengeance for Mako's death. There wasn't a human behind it, no one to blame. Just an even more confusing and ever-deepening mystery to solve . . .

Jake Pentecost, former star cadet and son of Jaeger pilot war hero Stacker Pentecost, makes a living in the criminal underworld of the Santa Monica slums.

Jake and his new friend Amara, an orphan who grew up in the streets of Santa Monica, get into trouble when they steal a valuable piece from a scrapped Jaeger. Using her homemade Jaeger, Scrapper, they put up a valiant fight before they're caught by the PPDC.

Jake's adoptive sister, Mako Mori, who followed in their father's footsteps to become a PPDC hero, gives Jake two choices: Go to jail or rejoin the PPDC as a Ranger to train new recruit Amara and the other cadets. Jake reluctantly accepts her offer.

Amara meets the other cadets and struggles to fit in at first. She has a lot to learn about becoming a cadet, and who not to pick a fight with!

Jake reunites with his old friend and former copilot, Nathan Lambert. Nathan isn't pleased to see Jake at first, still upset about a falling-out they had as cadets 11 years before.

A mysterious rogue Jaeger, Obsidian Fury, attacks PPDC headquarters in Sydney, causing massive destruction.

Jake and Nathan head to Siberia. Together, they pilot Gipsy Avenger and defeat Obsidian Fury after an intense battle.

Prominent tech executive Shao Liwen unveils her plan to replace piloted Jaegers with drones that can be safely controlled remotely from anywhere in the world.

During delivery of the Shao drones, they are hacked and begin attacking the PPDC, destroying Jaegers and Shatterdomes around the Pacific Rim.

The drone Kaiju begin opening multiple breaches around the world.

Three Kaiju make it through the breach heading towards Tokyo. Jake and Lambert assemble a team of humanity's last hopes to save the world: the cadets.

In the aftermath of all the destruction, they deploy the remaining Jaegers and launch into action.

When it looks like the Jaegers are winning the battle, the three Kaiju turn the tables by combining together into one gigantic Mega-Kaiju!

When Nathan is injured, Amara comes to Jake's rescue to copilot Gipsy Avenger, the last standing Jaeger. At the last minute, they're able to work together to destroy the mega-Kaiju and save the world.

Finally living up to his father's heroic legacy, Jake realizes that he was always destined for greatness as a Jaeger Pilot.

08

Jake and Nate stood inside Gottlieb's lab. Gottlieb set a goo-dripping chain saw down and peeled off his thick industrial rubber gloves.

"It's definitely Kaiju," he said. "A secondary brain. Used to control the hindquarters."

"Like the dinosaurs?" asked Nate.

"Actually, that's a persistent myth. Sauropods did have a sacra-lumbar expansion that was once thought—"

"How'd it get into our world?" interrupted Jake.

"Hasn't been a breach in ten years. Sensors would have picked it up," said Marshal Quan.

"I don't think there *was* a breach. Kaiju flesh has a distinct radioactive half-life signature, particular to the Anteverse. This specimen doesn't," said Gottlieb.

"You saying it came from *our* universe?" asked Nate.

"The genetic fingerprints indicate distinctly terrestrial modification techniques. Probably engineered from Kaiju tissue left over from the war," said Gottlieb.

Marshal Quan's eyes widened. "Precursors didn't do this. *Humans* did."

"How'd a bunch of crazy Kaiju worshippers do all that?" asked Jake.

"Doubtful they could have. Only a dozen or so biotech companies in the world could even take a run at it," said Gottlieb.

"We need to narrow that list down. *Fast*," commanded Quan.

Gottlieb got to work. Quan nodded at Jake and Nate. "Good work. Mako would be proud," he said. Then he distinctly turned to face Jake and said, "So would your father."

Jake's face twisted into thought. He wondered if his father would have echoed that sentiment.

Shatterdome security stood watch over Obsidian Fury, which lay broken and inert on the tarmac. Jules and a tech crew crawled over it like ants.

Amara, Jinhai, Meilin, and Suresh stared at Obsidian Fury in awe from across the tarmac.

"That hunk of Kaiju was part of a Jaeger?" asked Suresh.

"Really thought it was going to be ballerinas," said Jinhai.

Amara looked at the strange Jaeger, mesmerized. This was technological catnip to her. "We gotta get a look inside," she said.

"*Inside?*" asked Suresh.

"That thing's part Kaiju. Come on, guys. When are we ever going to get a chance to see something like this again?"

"Never. Never would be good," said Suresh.

"Stay here if you want. But I'm going," said Amara. Her eyes blazed with determination.

The group followed Amara. Their flashlights stabbed through the gloom.

Amara concentrated her light on the Kaiju tissue striated through the advanced Jaeger tech.

"It's fused all the way through the system. Like . . . muscle tissue," she observed.

"That's how it was able to move like it did. Cool," said Jinhai.

"Yeah, cool," said Suresh, who clearly wanted to get out of Obsidian as fast as possible.

An odd bundle of cables caught Amara's attention. "Shine your light over here," she said.

Jinhai aimed his flashlight at the cables as Amara wrestled to pull a cable loose.

"Oh, great, yeah. Let's go yanking on the guts of the weird Kaiju kill-bot," said Suresh.

Amara succeeded in ripping the cable loose. No one noticed that her yanking ruptured a Kaiju blood vessel running along the ceiling. She eyed the inside of the cable, her brow furrowing.

"What is it?" asked Jinhai.

Before she could answer, blue Kaiju blood dripped down. It just missed her—but it caught Jinhai in the arm! He grunted as the caustic blood ate through his jacket and seared his arm.

"Jinhai!" screamed Amara.

Jinhai dropped to the floor in agony, trying not to scream. Amara tore at his jacket, avoiding the caustic blood.

"I told you not to yank on those!" said Suresh.

"Go get help! Go!" said Amara. Meilin and Suresh bolted off.

Jinhai gripped Amara's arm, grunting in agony. Amara kneeled next to him, her face twisted in sorrow and fear.

Jake argued with Marshal Quan out in the corridor. Quan stormed off. Amara sat alone in the holding room. Jake walked in to talk to her.

"Is Jinhai okay?" she asked.

"There's gonna be some scarring, but yeah. He'll live," said Jake. "Marshal's put him on probation. Meilin and Suresh too. They blink wrong, all of 'em are out."

"It wasn't their fault. I talked them into it. Jake, listen, there's something—" Amara started, but Jake interrupted.

"Amara, I tried to talk to the marshal. I'm sorry. You're dismissed from the program," said Jake.

"Doesn't matter. Never belonged here anyway," said Amara.

Jake saw the pain her words attempted to cover. He crossed to sit next to her. "I said the same thing, long time ago. But I didn't *want* to be here. Not like you."

"Then why'd you sign up?" asked Amara.

"We were at war. My dad was leading the charge. I thought . . . I dunno. Maybe I'd see more of him. Maybe even drift with him . . ." Jake smiled. It was a happy memory.

"Then one night Nate—Ranger Lambert—and I get into it. Over something stupid, don't even remember what. So I climbed into an old Mark IV to show him I didn't need him or anybody else to be a great pilot."

Amara eyed him, stunned. "Wow. That was stupid."

Jake shook his head and laughed. "Yeah. Took two steps and blacked out from the strain. First thing I saw when I woke up in the infirmary was my dad. He told me I was out of the program. Said I didn't deserve to be in a Jaeger. He said—he said a lot of other things. And so did I. Soon as I could stand up, I left and never looked back."

Jake paused. A quiet moment passed. Then, he continued.

"A year later, he was gone. I never got the chance to prove him wrong. More importantly, I never got the chance to prove it to *myself*. Because I was angry. And hurt. Don't let what other people think define who you are. You won't like where that takes you. Do you understand? And keep your head up, and you might just be as good-looking as me in this type of situation. Seriously, this face is set up well. Beauty is a burden. You'll be alright."

Jake got up to leave. Amara stopped him.

"Shao Industries. That's what I was trying to tell you. Obsidian Fury has tech in it made by Shao Industries," she said.

"Jules and her team scanned every centimeter of that Jaeger. Didn't find any serial numbers or identifying markers," said Jake.

"Insulating metamaterials wound counterclockwise in the shunt cabling. Shao's the only company that winds them that way," explained Amara.

"Amara, are you sure?" asked Jake.

"Yeah. Stole a ton of it to make Scrapper. Thought it might be important," said Amara.

Jake tightened at the revelation. He rushed out of the holding cell.

It was night at the Moyulan Shatterdome. Jake, Nate, and Gottlieb hustled down the corridor.

"Shao Industries? They don't even have a bio division," said Gottlieb.

"That we know of," said Jake.

"Cabling could have been stolen, just like in Amara's Jaeger. We need more than that to link Obsidian Fury to Shao," said Nate.

"What about Newt? He'd have access to internal records, shipping manifests . . ." said Gottlieb.

"Go see him. Keep it low profile," said Jake.

"A mission. I have a secret mission!" said Gottlieb excitedly.

Amara sullenly looked on as PPDC security emptied out her locker in the cadet barracks.

"This isn't fair," said Suresh.

Jinhai stepped over with his arm bandaged from the Kaiju blood burn. "I tried to talk to my parents. But they wouldn't listen," he said.

"It was my 'mission.' This is on me," said Amara.

Security finished and started to lead Amara out of the barracks. Vik called to her, "*Amara*. The next Jaeger you build. Make it a *big* one," she said, supportively.

Amara nodded, choking back the emotion of leaving people she was beginning to feel were her family.

09

Shao Liwen strode through the lobby of her offices in Shanghai. It was time for drone deployment. Her eyes focused on a data pad in her hands. Chief Kang fell into step with her. "The building's secure, ma'am," he said.

"No visitors without the proper credentials. I don't want anyone interfering with deployment," said Shao.

Her data pad beeped. She eyed something on it and frowned—suspicion clouding her face.

Meanwhile, inside a remote room owned by Shao Industries, Newt worked a holo screen. He punched in commands to track the drones in the field.

". . . *aaaand* delivery at one hundred percent! That right there, that's the way you do it—" he said gleefully.

Warning lights flashed! Burke wrestled with his controls.

"Losing uplink to drone 375!" said Burke.

Newt whirled around as more warning lights flashed. Now several remote pilots lost their uplink connections.

At the Moyulan Shatterdome, Xiang tensed. A holo map of Jaegers in the field flashed red. Out on the tarmac, two drone Jaegers were being flown in via Jumphawks. Amara glanced up at them as PPDC security escorted her out.

Jake, heading to a Jumphawk with Nate and Quan, locked eyes with her across the tarmac.

"Give me a second," said Jake.

He started toward her, but an urgent comm stopped him.

"Marshal, the drones in the field are malfunctioning! We need to stop the ones coming in from deploying!" said Xiang over the comm.

"There's something wrong with the drones!" said Marshal Quan.

WHOOM! The drones being flown in lit up with Kaiju energy. Alien flesh stabbed out between their metal plates. They thrashed in midair, destroying their Jumphawks. Then they immediately unleashed a barrage of plasma missiles as they hit the ground!

"Get to Gipsy! Go!" screamed Marshal Quan.

Jake and Nate took off for Jaeger Bay.

"All pilots! Man your Jaegers and engage hostiles—" said Quan.

BOOM! The Kaiju drones destroyed Valor Omega. Debris cartwheeled across the tarmac. Amara dove out of the way as Valor Omega's severed head slammed into her PPDC security escort.

The Kaiju drones started blasting at everything in sight: Jumphawks, equipment, fleeing personnel. There was no remorse. Amara's eyes widened with the terror of war . . .

In Shanghai, the main building of Shao Industries erupted into chaos. Staff and techs rushed through the corridors. Newt hurried in the opposite direction of everyone else, mumbling to himself.

"Okay, okay, you got this, it's cool. You cool? Yeah, I'm cool. I'm super cool . . ." he said.

Qingsheng, one of the lab techs, shouted as he passed, "Dr. Geiszler! She's looking for you."

"I know! I know! I'm heading up!" said Newt.

Newt rounded the corner, and WHAM! Gottlieb yanked him aside.

"Hermann? How did you get in here?" asked Newt.

"I do have PPDC credentials—and besides, everyone here seems a bit preoccupied with the *killer drones your boss just set off,*" said Gottlieb.

"It's not her fault!" said Newt. "Maybe they found a way to hack—"

"This has nothing to do with Kaiju worshippers!" said Gottlieb. "We found evidence linking Obsidian Fury to Shao Industries."

"This Shao Industries?"

"No, the Shao Industries that makes knickerbocker glories. Yes, this one. I came to see if you would help corroborate from the inside, but now that Shao has shown her hand with these drones—"

"Why would she build drones to go bananas and attack?" asked Newt. "It doesn't make any sense. And what in the world is a knickerbocker glory?"

"She used you. Lured you with money and a fancy title. And while you were basking in the glow, she took your research and twisted it," Gottlieb hissed at Newt as they walked through the corridor.

Newt chewed his lip. His eyes flicked around nervously.

"You really believe that?" he asked.

"It's not your fault. She's been playing all of us. Help me stop her, Newton. Help me save the world, like old times," said Gottlieb.

"Well, you were technically helping *me* last time—" said Newt.

"Fine. Help me help *you* save the world. What do you say?" asked Gottlieb.

Newt wrestled with that. An internal conflict raged inside him.

"I say—DON'T SHOOT!" said Newt.

He threw his hands up. Chief Kang and his men rushed in with their guns drawn. Shao had found them.

At Jaeger Bay, explosions boomed from the tarmac. Amara rushed alongside with a flood of other personnel. Jinhai, Vik, Meilin, Suresh, Ilya, Tahima, Renata, and Ryoichi intercepted her.

"What's happening?" asked Jinhai.

"Are those Jaegers?" asked Ryoichi.

"Drones, from Shao Industries!" said Amara.

"What are they doing?" asked Tahima.

"I don't know! They just went crazy!" said Amara.

Jake and Nate hustled past, dodging debris as they tried to get to Gipsy Avenger.

"Clear the deck!" ordered Nate.

"Get to your quarters!" said Jake.

Boom! Plasma missiles slammed into Titan Redeemer as she came out of her dock. The blast crippled her leg. Thrown off balance, Titan Redeemer groaned and teetered over them.

"Go! Go!" Nate shouted, as he and Jake tried to get the cadets out of the way of the falling Jaeger. But Nate didn't clear in time. Falling metal was about to hit him when . . .

WHAM! Jules tackled him out of the way just as Titan slammed to the ground. She lay on top of him as the shockwave hit.

"Hey," said Jules affectionately.

"Hey," said Nate back.

Jake frowned in disbelief at the timing. "Seriously? *Now?*" he asked.

Back in Shanghai, Newt and Gottlieb were in an elevator surrounded by Shao security. Newt caught Gottlieb's attention, and shot his eyebrow toward Gottlieb's cane. Gottlieb frowned, confused. Newt motioned at the cane again. Gottlieb understood. He coughed, half doubling over.

Then he swung his cane! It broke a guard's nose. Newt grabbed Kang as the chief whipped out his sidearm.

Shots rang out! Then DING! The door opened right as Newt smashed Kang in the face with his own sidearm. Newt and Gottlieb dashed out, leaving behind a pile of unconscious officers.

"Thank you, Newton! I'd hug you if I didn't have a rule about public displays of affection—oh to hell with it!" said Gottlieb. Then, he hugged Newt. Newt was surprised at the gesture.

"You're welcome, Hermann. Now if you're done groping me, we need to take care of these drones," he said.

They burst into the lab at Shao Industries, where everything had been thrown into chaos. Newt waved the gun he took from Kang.

"Out!" he said. Then in Mandarin, "Go! Now!"

The lab techs fled. Daiyu shouted at Newt as he dashed out, "Always knew you'd go crazy!"

"You're fired!" said Newt.

"What do we do? How do we stop this?" asked Gottlieb.

"Back door!" said Newt.

Newt set the gun down as he rushed to a terminal and punched in commands.

"To what? The lab?" asked Gottlieb.

A holo screen flared to life. The Kaiju drones were pinpointed around the Pacific Rim.

Newt kept inputting commands. "To the drone subroutine," he said. "I slipped one in just in case I wanted to get in there and poke around down the road."

"Sneaky!" said Gottlieb.

"I know, right?" replied Newt.

Then he stabbed enter. But the Kaiju drones didn't deactivate. Instead, an ominous message flashed across the holo screen: COMND LIMA VICTOR 426 CONFIRMED. INITIATING BREACH PROTOCOL.

Gottlieb's face dropped. "What did you just do?" he asked.

"What I've been planning for the last ten years. Ending

the world," said Newt. Then he grinned. Something dark and malicious welled in his eyes. Gottlieb stiffened in horror. It wasn't Shao Liwen who was behind all of this. It was *Newt*!

10

A Kaiju Jaeger emerged from the ocean, joining four more that gathered just off the shore of the Santa Monica slums. They formed a circle as blue-tinged particle beams erupted from their chest reactors. The beams slammed together in a thunderclap of raw energy. The water between them churned. They were opening a breach!

At the Moyulan Shatterdome, Marshal Quan rushed to the command center, a bit roughed up from his journey. "Where are my pilots?"

Red circles popped up across a holo screen map. Kaiju drones were opening up breaches all around the Pacific Rim!

"Breaches detected! Multiple locations! It's the drones, sir!" said Xiang.

Quan's eyes widened in shock. "All pilots! Breaches detected! Drones in the field—" said Quan over the comms.

But suddenly, plasma missiles screamed over Jake and slammed into the command center. Quan and everyone inside were annihilated. Jake, Jules, and Nate dove behind Titan Redeemer as the building crashed down.

In the lab, Gottlieb eyed the breaches on Newt's holo screen in complete horror.

"Why? Why would you do this?" he asked.

"He wouldn't. Or maybe he would. Maybe he hates all of you. For laughing at him. For treating him like an insignificant little joke of a man." The words came out of Newt's mouth, but the message seemed to be from someone else.

Then a shock of recognition slammed Gottlieb.

"You . . ." he said.

Behind Newt's eyes, Gottlieb glimpsed the insect-like alien nightmares that were controlling Newt.

"*Precursors,*" said Gottlieb.

Newt twitched. The malevolence in his eyes was replaced by fear as he struggled to break free of the mental hold.

"Help me, Hermann. They're in my head . . ." said Newt.

"Fight them, Newton! Fight them—" said Gottlieb. He remembered how awful—how powerful—the Kaiju's mental control had been when he and Newt drifted with the Kaiju during the war. Newt must have never broken completely free from it.

Newt spasmed. The Precursors clamped down. He backhanded Gottlieb, sending him crashing against a lab table.

"He isn't strong enough. None of you are," said the Precursors.

The sound of a bullet being chambered split the air. Newt whirled. Shao had slipped into the lab—and she had the gun Newt had set down leveled right at him. Newt chuckled, unfazed.

"Hey, boss. Finally figured it out, huh? What was it? The diagnostics?"

"My numbers weren't aligning with yours. How did you do it without me knowing?" asked Shao.

"Thirty-eight percent of your company is fully automated. Wasn't that difficult to reallocate a little here and there over the years without being detected." Then Newt switched to perfect Mandarin: "Especially since you always thought you were the smartest one in the room."

"In about half a second, I'm going to be," said Shao.

She squeezed the trigger and BLAM! Gottlieb knocked her hand up with his cane, causing the shot to go wide.

Newt tossed Gottlieb into Shao and ran. They went

down in a tumble. Shao whipped the gun up but Gottlieb grabbed her arm.

"Stop! It isn't him! It's the Precursors! They must have infected his mind when we drifted with a Kaiju brain during the—"

"Shut up. And don't ever touch me again," said Shao. She stabbed an intercom on Newt's holo terminal. "Security, find and detain Dr. Geiszler. If he tries to resist, do whatever you need to do to stop him."

Explosions rocked the bay outside the Moyulan Shatterdome. Amara, Jinhai, Vik, Ryoichi, Suresh, Ilya, and Renata rushed to join Jake, Jules, and Nate. They all took cover behind Titan Redeemer.

"We told you to get to quarters!" said Jake.

"Corridor's blocked!" said Amara.

"Where's Tahima and Meilin?" asked Nate.

"I don't know!" said Amara.

"What do we do?" asked Renata.

"Stay here. We're going to try to get to Gipsy," said Jake.

Explosions rocked the bay between them and Gipsy.

Jake shared a look with Nate. Chances of making it weren't on their side.

"You ready for this?" asked Jake.

"No. You?" said Nate.

"Nope. On three. One, two—"

They tensed to run into the inferno of destruction when suddenly Gottlieb's voice came over the comm: "—ello? Anyone there?"

"Gottlieb?" said Jake.

Shao worked Newt's holo screen. Her fingers flew as Gottlieb spoke into a comm at a nearby terminal.

"Jake, thank goodness! I've been trying to reach the command center—" said Gottlieb.

"It's gone! We're under attack! You have to force Shao to shut down the drones!"

"It isn't her," said Gottlieb. "It was Newt. Precursors infected him and got into his head."

"Gottlieb, it's me," said Nate. "Can you make him disable the drones?"

"No. He—he got away. It was my fault. I—" started Gottlieb. But then the holo screen suddenly shifted. Data blocks smashed aside.

"I've penetrated the subroutine. Initiating shutdown protocol," said Shao.

The Kaiju drones stormed into Jaeger Bay, blasting everything in sight. Jake shouted into his comm. "Shut 'em down!"

"Stand by," said Gottlieb.

Shao's fingers flashed across the holo screen. The shutdown protocol was unresponsive! The smashed data blocks started reforming.

"It's trying to lock you out," said Gottlieb.

Shao had an idea. "*Feedback loop.*"

Her fingers flew, racing against the closing data blocks.

"Brilliant! If you modify that algorithm—" said Gottlieb.

"*Gottlieb,*" said Nate.

"Stand by," he responded.

"Gottlieb, shut 'em down now or we're all gonna die!" said Jake. A shadow fell over him. He whipped his eyes up to see a Kaiju drone leveling its weapons to obliterate the group.

SCREECH! The Kaiju drone staggered as it got hit by Shao's feedback loop. Inside the drone, the Kaiju brain violently vibrated. Then it exploded!

The Kaiju drone keeled over, and so did its counterparts across the bay. Every one of them collapsed, their particle beams flaring out. On the holo screen, breaches winked out, one after another.

"Yes!" shouted Gottlieb. "Jake! Shao disabled the drones! The breaches are closed—"

All of a sudden, three blinking circles appeared on the holo screen along with the words: KAIJU DETECTED.

"Oh no," said Gottlieb.

Jake rose. Jaeger Bay was smoldering around him. "Oh no, what? Gottlieb?"

"Three Kaiju have gotten through. South Korea, Russian coast, East China Sea. Two Cat IVs and a Cat V."

Everyone registered the severity of this.

"Copy that," said Jake. "Get back to the 'dome. We're gonna need all the help we can get."

At Shao Industries, Gottlieb eyed the blinking circles that indicated the Kaiju. They were already on the move!

Jules hustled through the devastation at Jaeger Bay. Techs assessed damage while medics tended to the wounded, including Meilin. Jake and Nate helped Amara, Jinhai, and Vik lift the hunk of concrete that was pinning down Tahima. Jules rushed over.

"Medic!" screamed Jules.

A medic dashed to Tahima's side.

Nate looked at Jules. "What do you got?"

"Reports are still coming in, but drones took out Jaegers and Shatterdomes across the Rim," said Jules.

"How many Jaegers we have here?" asked Jake.

"Operational? Gipsy Avenger. Barely."

"That's it?" asked Nate.

"Have to get more up and running or it's gonna be a short fight," said Jake.

"Even if we can, all our other pilots are—" said Jules.

"One disaster at a time. Let's focus on those Jaegers," said Nate.

Jake looked at Amara. "Think you can help with the repairs?"

"Me? Thought I was kicked out," she said.

"I'm kicking you back in. Nobody has more experience turning junk into Jaegers," said Jake. Then he looked at Nate. "You good with that?"

Nate eyed Amara and grinned in support. He knew how valuable she was to the corps. "Outstanding," said Nate.

Amara felt a rush of strength from the rangers' support. Then Jinhai interrupted. "We got incoming!" he said, pointing at the tarmac.

The group rushed to the tarmac to see a small army of high-tech aircrafts land. The Shao Industries logo was written across them. A beaming Gottlieb leapt out with Shao Liwen right behind him. Chief Kang and his men followed. They were all battered and bruised from their run-in with Newt.

"I brought some help!" said Gottlieb.

An army of Shao Industries technicians and equipment poured out from the V-Dragons. Jake grinned, relieved to see backup. The group headed to the war room.

There, they gathered around a holo screen, tracking the destructive path of the three Kaiju.

"Hakuja. Shrikethorn. And the big fellow, Raijin. I took the liberty of assigning designations," said Gottlieb.

"Yeah, great names. Sound like real jerks," said Jake.

"Shrikethorn and Raijin are moving away from the cities, toward the ocean," said Nate.

"Maybe they're trying to link up with Hakuja in the East China Sea," said Shao.

"Newt would know what they're up to, if we could get it out of him," said Jake.

"Have to find him first," said Nate.

Shao's eyes darkened at the mention of the man who betrayed her—and all of humanity.

"He escaped in a Shao V-Dragon," she said. "My men are trying to track him, but he disabled the transponder."

"Then that's off the table. Any Jaegers closer to those Kaiju than us?" asked Jake.

"What was left from the Chin-do and Sakhalinsk 'domes tried to intercept. Emphasis on *tried*," said Gottlieb.

"There's gotta be something there. Something in the East China Sea," said Nate.

Jake tensed as he realized what was happening. "Maybe that's not where they're headed. Pull up a map of Kaiju movement from the war," he said to Gottlieb.

"You know something we don't?" asked Nate.

"You said you have to understand your enemy's objective to know you've beaten them," said Jake. A map displaying Kaiju incursions from the war appeared. "What if the Kaiju weren't blindly attacking our cities during the war?" Jake worked the screen, extrapolating where the Kaiju would have gone if they hadn't been stopped. "What if we were just *in their way*?"

The extrapolation lines intersected at a single point!

"Mount Fuji, Japan," said Nate.

Gottlieb extrapolated the lines for the three Kaiju out there: Hakuja, Shrikethorn, and Raijin. Their paths also intersected at the same coordinates.

"Mount Fuji. But why?" asked Shao.

Gottlieb stiffened in horror, suddenly understanding. "Rare earth elements. Mount Fuji is a volcano rich in *rare earth elements*. Kaiju blood reacts violently with them. It's the basis of my thruster fuel experiments."

"That sounds bad. That's bad, right?" asked Nate.

"Very. Mount Fuji is *active*. A geological pressure point," said Shao.

Gottlieb worked the holo screen. "Based on the blood to mass ratio of the Kaiju... the reaction would cause a cascade event, igniting the Ring of Fire around the Pacific Rim."

Graphics showed all the volcanoes compromising the Pacific Rim's Ring of Fire erupting in succession. A massive cloud spread over the entire earth.

"Billions of tons of toxic gas and ash will spew into the atmosphere, wiping out all life," said Gottlieb, swallowing hard.

"And finish terraforming Earth for the Precursors," said Shao.

"This doesn't make any sense. Why not just open a breach right over Fuji and drop the Kaiju in?" asked Nate.

"Or send one so big nothing could stop it?" asked Jake.

"From the data we recovered from Dr. Geiszler's files, the Precursors can only penetrate dimensional 'soft spots' between universes. Every location the drones chose corresponded to one of these," said Shao.

"And a Category V is theoretically the largest Kaiju they could send through, since the energy it takes to widen a breach exponentially quadruples—" said Gottlieb.

"Yeah, science is our friend, we get it," said Jake.

"We can't let them reach Mount Fuji," said Nate.

"I'll check with Jules, see where we are with the Jaeger repairs," said Jake.

"Even if you had a hundred, there's no way to intercept in time. The drones destroyed your Jumphawks, and my V-Dragons aren't built to carry that kind of load," said Shao.

"What about your thruster pods?" Nate asked Gottlieb.

"They're not ready," said Gottlieb.

"Can they be?" asked Shao.

"In theory, maybe, with your help," said Gottlieb.

"What does that mean, *in theory?*" asked Jake.

Gottlieb straightened with determination. "Today it means *yes.*"

11

A huge carrier truck hauled a gigantic container of Kaiju blood from a bay across from where the Jaegers were housed. Gottlieb oversaw the transfer.

Jules directed an enormous crane as it lifted Titan Redeemer's mace arm into the air to be used as parts to repair damaged Jaegers.

Inside Bracer Phoenix's head, Amara and Jinhai wrestled to get Bracer's inner "ear" mechanism back in place. It almost tumbled, but Vik rushed in and helped them secure it. Jinhai worked an impact wrench to bolt the piece in place as Amara exited through the conn-pod hatch and out onto the catwalk. She paused to tell Suresh and Ilya what to do with a stack of machine parts. They hoisted a heavy piece, carrying it to Bracer Phoenix.

Renata and Ryoichi were suspended by repelling harnesses as they welded a plate closed on Saber's chest. Every one of the cadets was working hard!

A small army of J-Techs and Shao techs were also

suspended near them, repairing the damaged Jaeger. Renata paused to wipe sweat from her eyes and made the mistake of looking down. They were a long, long way off the ground.

Jake and Nate helped Shao techs load a hunk of salvaged machinery onto a scrambler. Jake thumped the side, giving them the signal to drive off. He nodded to Shao as she passed. She absently returned the nod, her fingers flying across a data pad.

Shao spotted Gottlieb entering from the tarmac and excitedly joined him to show him her calculations. Gottlieb scanned the data pad, his eyes brightening with the light of discovery.

Shao worked the holo display, trying to get Gottlieb's fuel equation to balance. She failed, then tried again. It locked into place!

She threw an excited look to Gottlieb who worked at the main vid screen. He rushed over, confirming the equation at a terminal near Shao. His crazy idea was going to work! Probably. Maybe . . .

Jules updated Jake and Nate as they hustled toward Gipsy.

"Saber Athena, Guardian Bravo, and Bracer Phoenix are good to go," she said.

"Not a lot to work with," said Jake.

"Shao's team kit-bashed some Fury tech into Gipsy that might help," said Jules.

"Prep everything we've got for deployment," said Nate.

"Don't get yourself hurt, okay?" Jules said to Nate. She kissed him on the cheek.

Then she turned to Jake. "You either," she said. She also kissed him on the cheek, and then headed off down the corridor. Jake and Nate both watched her go.

"Well that's confusing," said Jake.

Nate frowned in agreement. "Let's stay on point," he said. "We only have four Jaegers. Against two Category IVs and a fiver."

"Better than just Gipsy," said Jake.

"Still need pilots," said Nate.

"We have them," said Jake.

Nate realized whom Jake was referring to and exhaled in concern. Were the cadets ready for this?

Amara, Jinhai, Vik, Suresh, Ilya, Renata, and Ryoichi lined up in their cadet drivesuits, helmets in hand. Jake and Nate were now in their ranger drivesuits, too. Jake nodded to the nervous cadets, reassuring them and himself.

"If my dad were here, he'd probably give a big speech, make you all feel invincible," said Jake. "But I'm not my father. I'm not . . . I'm not a hero like he was. Like Raleigh Becket and Mako Mori. But they didn't start out that way. They started as *cadets*, just like you. We remember them as giants because they stood tall. Because they stood *together*. It doesn't matter how many tries it took to get here. Or who your parents are. Or where you came from. Or who believed in you and who didn't. You're part of a family now."

Jake glanced to Nate, remembering his own speech to the cadets in the sim room.

"This is *our* time. This is *our* chance to make a difference," said Jake. "Mount up and let's get it done."

The cadets straightened with pride and determination.

12

Inside Bracer Phoenix, Amara, Jinhai, and Vik climbed into their drift cradles. Amara and Jinhai were up front with Vik in the back.

"Initiating neural handshake . . ." said Amara.

The three reacted as their minds opened to each other. Jinhai grinned at the readout on his display. "Neural handshake strong and steady," he said.

"So. How's it feel to be in a *real* Jaeger?" Vik asked Amara.

"Bigger's . . . not bad," said Amara.

Then all three of them grinned.

Inside Gipsy Avenger, Nate and Jake were in their drift cradles, finishing their predeployment check.

Nate addressed the squad over the comm. "All Jaegers, sound off, go-no-go for launch."

"Suresh and Ilya—" said Nate.

"Guardian Bravo. Go," they responded.

"Renata and Ryoichi—" said Nate.

"Saber Athena. Go," they responded.

"Amara, Jinhai, and Vik," said Nate.

"Bracer Phoenix. Let's go already," said Amara.

"Copy that. Command, we are go for launch," said Jake.

Gipsy and the other three Jaegers stood on their launch pads. Gottlieb eyed them from the main holo screen, where he was overseeing the launch with his new thruster pods. Jules hustled in past war room techs that were working the support terminals, and she took a position across from Gottlieb.

"Roger, Gipsy Avenger. Ignition in ten seconds," said Gottlieb. Then he started to count down.

"9 . . . 8 . . ."

The cadets were apprehensive but eager.

"7 . . . 6 . . . 5 . . . 4 . . ."

Jake and Nate tensed as the countdown lowered.

"3 . . . 2 . . . 1 . . . ignition!"

BOOM! Kaiju-blue tinted flames erupted from the thruster pods. The Jaegers started to rise on pillars of flame and smoke. Inside, the conn-pods shook violently, like they were about to come apart. The cadets looked like they were about to puke.

Warning alarms blared. Suresh swallowed hard. "That's not a good sound!"

Even Jake and Nate exchanged nervous glances. "Come on, girl. Hold together . . ." said Jake.

Gipsy, Bracer, Guardian, and Saber launched triumphantly into the sky!

Jules and the rest of the war room cheered. Gottlieb exhaled in relief, grinning weakly at Jules. "Knew it would work," he said.

Raijin, Hakuja, and Shrikethorn rampaged through the megacity of Tokyo. People on the street were running to the nearest Kaiju shelters.

Raijin paused as he spied something up ahead. He roared at Hakuja and Shrikethorn. The Kaiju were communicating! These weren't mindless beasts. They were intelligent and working together.

Mount Fuji loomed in the distance. Raijin started for it, with Hakuja and Shrikethorn following.

Whomp! Gipsy Avenger dropped out of the sky. Her thruster pods dropped out as she landed on Raijin and threw the Kaiju into a building. She skidded to a stop and rose.

"Gipsy to Command. Targets acquired," said Nate.

"Um. Roger that, Gipsy," said Gottlieb.

Gottlieb worked the holo screen, scanning the city for people. The scan came up negative.

"Everyone in the city is secured in underground shelters. You're cleared to engage."

"Solid copy. Going hot," said Jake.

Guardian Bravo, Saber Athena, and Bracer Phoenix rocketed down, backing Gipsy up.

Jake spoke into the comms: "Bracer Phoenix, on me. We'll take Raijin. Saber Athena, Guardian Bravo, you take the other two."

"Copy that," said Suresh. "We were born to save the world."

"On my mark. Three, two, one—*mark*!" said Nate.

Amara tightened with determination as they hurled into battle. The four Jaegers stormed down the empty streets toward the three Kaiju.

Saber was the fastest in the fleet and surged ahead. She whipped out plasma swords from her back and attacked Hakuja. Hakuja tried to counter, but Saber spin-kicked the Kaiju in the face, sending it crashing back!

Gipsy streaked past the fallen monster. She reared back her truck-sized fist and launched it at Raijin.

Armored plates suddenly snapped closed around the Kaiju's head, protecting it. Gipsy's fist connected with the plates and WHOOM! The kinetic force from the hit was absorbed and transferred in a flash of energy to Raijin's claws.

Raijin roared! Its superpowered claws raked across Gipsy and sent her flying back. Bracer ducked just as Gipsy sailed back overhead.

Gipsy crashed against the side of a building. Bracer continued on, firing missiles as she barreled toward Raijin. Raijin roared and backhanded Bracer, sending her sailing through a building.

In Guardian Bravo, Suresh and Ilya ran full tilt toward Shrikethorn, firing missiles. But Bracer Phoenix landed right in Guardian Bravo's path. Guardian tumbled to the ground and skidded to a stop, his giant metal fist just bumping an abandoned car. Its alarm went off.

Gipsy started to rise, finally recovered from Raijin's superpowered blow.

Gottlieb eyed Raijin's data streaming across a holo display. "Gipsy! Raijin's faceplates are absorbing your hits and throwing the energy back at you!" he said over the comms.

Jake and Nate regained their senses. "Let's see it absorb *this*," said Jake. He activated the gravity sling. The sling latched onto a building, and he yanked it down on top of Raijin. Raijin shook it off and kept coming!

Gipsy pulled another building down on Raijin. And another. And another. But the Kaiju was unstoppable! Jake and Nate strained with all their might to pull another building down on the unstoppable Raijin.

One street over, Hakuja recovered. The Kaiju tensed to pounce on Gipsy Avenger but WHAM! Saber Athena hit Hakuja with a flying knee, driving the Kaiju's head into a building! Hakuja surged up and Saber attacked again, pummeling the beast.

Gipsy gravity-slung another building down on Raijin. The beast staggered, but it kept coming.

Guardian started to rise as Shrikethorn rounded the corner two streets away from Saber. Shrikethorn launched armored quills from its tail at Saber. The quills smashed into Saber, ripping at the Jaeger's metal body.

Renata and Ryoichi grunted in pain as holographic quills smashed into them. Hakuja seized the distraction and leapt onto Saber, driving her back into a Kaiju museum. Renata and Ryoichi struggled to keep Hakuja's snapping jaws from ripping them apart. Ryoichi spotted Shrikethorn on its way to help Hakuja.

"Shrikethorn inbound!" said Ryoichi.

"Hey guys! We could use a little help over here!" said Renata.

"Copy that!" said Amara.

Amara, Jinhai, and Vik rose inside Bracer. They had only just recovered from the hit they took from Raijin.

"Vik! Take out Shrikethorn!" said Amara.

"On it!" said Vik. The floor under her drift cradle opened and she dropped down into position behind mounted rail guns that swiveled 360 degrees around the Jaeger's midsection. She opened fire on Shrikethorn!

Bracer's rail guns tore into Shrikethorn. The Kaiju bellowed in pain and turned away from Saber and Hakuja to face Bracer.

Suresh and Ilya ran as fast as they could to help Saber.

"Saber Athena! Guardian Bravo coming to assist!" said Suresh.

"Activating arc whip!" said Ilya.

Power surged inside their conn-pod. Guardian Bravo

unleashed an unbreakable graphene arc whip that crackled with energy! She leapt into the air.

Ilya and Suresh snapped the holographic whip in midair, and it slashed Hakuja across the back! Hakuja roared and let go of Saber.

Guardian landed, spun, and unleashed a devastating blow with the arc whip. Hakuja smashed through a building! The Kaiju bellowed angrily. Then, it burrowed into the ground.

"Yeah, that's right! You better run!" said Suresh. Then looking at Ilya, "These things ain't that tough!"

Gipsy, who was still pulling buildings down on Raijin, was knocked off-balance when Hakuja passed underground beneath her.

On the next street over, Bracer managed to drive Shrikethorn back with her rail guns.

Jake tensed as he spotted Hakuja's designator on Gipsy's screen. The Kaiju was moving underground toward Bracer Phoenix.

"Bracer, check your six! Hostile inbound!" said Jake into the comms.

"Copy that!" said Vik. She punched her holo screen, and

her turret suddenly rotated and swiveled around to Bracer's back just as Hakuja burst out of the ground behind them. Vik opened up with the rail gun, blasting Hakuja point-blank in the face. Vik hooted with adrenaline-pumping joy.

"Yeah! Get some!" she said gleefully.

Gipsy toppled another building onto Raijin with her gravity sling. Raijin shrieked this time, momentarily trapped. Gipsy took advantage and unleashed a barrage of plasma missiles at the Kaiju.

Saber stormed past and attacked Shrikethorn. Bracer continued blasting Hakuja with her rail guns. The Kaiju were on the ropes!

Drenched in sweat, with grease all over her, Shao eyed a holo screen. "They're winning," she said, in disbelief.

"That's what we do," said Gottlieb. "Most of the time."

13

The holo screen flickered in the war room. The data from the battle was replaced by Newt speaking into his data pad's camera from the Tokyo rooftop.

"Hey buddy. Moshi moshi," said Newt.

"*Newton*," exclaimed Gottlieb.

"So you finally figured out your little rockets. Good for you, Hermann," said Newt.

"That's not all we've figured out," said Gottlieb.

"We know what you're trying to do," said Jules.

"It's not him. It's those things in his head," said Gottlieb.

"Everybody has things in their head. Mine are just a lot more fun," said Newt.

"I've been in your mind, too, Newton. You're stronger than they know," said Gottlieb.

Newt twitched, his real self trying to break through. "I couldn't stop drifting with the Kaiju brain. I tried but she made me feel so . . . *alive*. They're in my mind. They're controlling me. I'm sorry, Hermann."

Newt jerked, the Precursors seizing control again. "Nice try. You don't even know what this is. How all the pieces fit together. Want me to show you? Want to see what else I was whipping up in Siberia? Yes? No? How 'bout yes."

Newt pushed a button on his data pad screen with flourish. "This is gonna be so cool. I mean, not for you guys. For you it's gonna suck. Sorry. But not really."

Newt disconnected. Lance Corporal McKinney tensed as her tactical screen flashed. "We got movement! Multiple hostiles! Three kilometers, southeast!" she said.

McKinney swiped the intel to the main holo screen. Little red dots clustered near the raging battle sprang to life.

"Command to strike team. Are you reading this?" said Gottlieb into the comms.

Gipsy Avenger's display lit up as it zeroed in on the rippers.

"Where'd they come from?" asked Jake.

Shao looked at the holo display and tensed. "That's one of my automated factories," she said.

SCREECH! The rippers—biomechanical, tentacled nightmares the size of SUVs—surged down the street, sending cars flying.

Gipsy's holo screens flashed, indicating rippers surging toward their position.

"It was Newt! Triangulating his signal—" said Nate.

Jake spoke into the comms: "All Jaegers, disengage from Kaiju and brace for contact!

Gipsy, Bracer, Guardian, and Saber disengaged from the battered Kaiju and turned to face the tidal wave of rippers hurtling toward them.

Newt tracked the ripper swarm on his data pad from the rooftop. Just as they were about to slam into the Jaegers, he swiped his data pad, abruptly changing the rippers' course.

Instead of attacking Gipsy, Bracer, Guardian, and Saber, the rippers swarmed the Kaiju! The Kaiju roared in agony as they fell down. The rippers tore into their flesh.

Ilya shared a confused look with Suresh.

Gottlieb and Jules tensed as the Kaiju and ripper indicators on their holo screen began to coalesce. The rippers weren't defeating the Kaiju—they were stitching the three Kaijus' flesh together to make one massive Kaiju monster!

The mega-Kaiju rose. Two Category IVs and a Category V joined together into one multitailed, metal-enhanced monster nightmare. Its head literally scraped the clouds and blocked the sun!

Jake and Nate felt shock course through them as they stared at the abomination that now loomed over them.

Newt grinned. "This is the way the world ends. Not with a whimper. But with a *bang*. A very, very big bang," he said to himself.

The mega-Kaiju roared! Windows across the city shattered. The monster lumbered toward the Jaegers, toppling buildings with its ripper-encrusted tail as it moved.

"All Jaegers, advance and fire everything you've got!" said Jake.

Gipsy Avenger rushed forward. She fired everything she had at the mega-Kaiju! The cadet-piloted Jaegers flanking her did the same. Missiles, particle beams, and plasma blasts all slammed into the gigantic beast!

But the ripper plating absorbed and deflected all the hits. The mega-Kaiju roared and smashed a giant fist into the ground. The shock wave threw the Jaegers into the air!

The Jaegers crashed to the ground—but Guardian Bravo miraculously landed on its feet. Ilya and Suresh surged forward to attack the mega-Kaiju.

Jake and Nate struggled to get up. "Guardian, stand down!" screamed Jake into the comms.

"We got this!" said Ilya.

"Go for the eyes!" said Suresh.

"Which ones?" said Ilya.

"All of them!"

The mega-Kaiju slammed the ground again but Guardian leapt up, kicking off a building as he swung his arc whip.

The mega-Kaiju caught the whip. It swung Guardian around and then smashed the Jaeger through a set of buildings.

Suresh and Ilya desperately hung on to the arc whip.

Newt watched as the mega-Kaiju hurled Guardian across the city. Guardian crashed into a final skyscraper that collapsed on top of the critically damaged Jaeger.

Newt laughed at how easily his creation took out Jake and his team. The mega-Kaiju headed for Mount Fuji!

14

Jake and Nate wrestled to stabilize Gipsy. Their Jaeger had taken a serious blow and their conn-pod showed it.

"Guardian Bravo, sitrep! You guys okay?" asked Nate.

Nothing but static came over the receiver.

"Ilya. Suresh. Report!" Jake said with urgency.

Ilya lay bloodied and dazed, tangled in the wreckage of the conn-pod. He weakly clicked his comm on. "Guardian's down. I'm pinned in the conn-pod. Suresh—"

His voice broke as he glanced over to his copilot. "Suresh didn't make it, sir."

The news hit Jake and Nate hard. It was terrible enough when a battle-tested pilot fell, but Suresh was only a cadet—young and not trained for this kind of battle. They felt the pain of losing him deeply.

"Copy, Guardian," said Jake.

"We'll send help soon as we can," said Nate.

"Bracer Phoenix, report," said Jake.

Amara and Jinhai tried to process the loss of one of

their own. "We're a little banged up, but still in the fight," said Amara.

"Us, too," said Renata. She and Ryoichi struggled to keep it together after hearing the news about Suresh. "S-Saber I mean. Saber Athena, sir," she said.

Jake permitted himself a moment of relief, taking whatever miracles he could get. He punched coordinates.

"Bracer, Saber, prepare to intercept at the following coordinates," he said.

Amara's eyes gleamed. It was time for payback.

Gipsy Avenger took off across the city. Bracer Phoenix and Saber Athena followed suit. Guardian Bravo lay weakly in the rubble. She began to stir, struggling to rise.

"Sir. I'm gonna try to pilot Guardian myself," said Ilya over the comms.

"Negative. Stand down, Cadet," ordered Nate.

Ilya strained in his drift cradle. "I can help, sir—"

"Ilya, stand *down*. That's an order!" said Jake.

Ilya ripped off his helmet, frustrated and angry.

"We know how bad you want back in the fight, but even a seasoned vet can't pilot a Jaeger without help—" said Jake. Then he tensed. An idea struck him.

"Gipsy to Command. Do you have a tactical scan of the hostile?" asked Jake.

McKinney hurriedly pulled up data on her tactical display and pushed it to the main holo screen. "Assessing data from their sensors . . ." she said.

A partial scan of the mega-Kaiju appeared on the holo screen.

"We have it, Gipsy, but it's still compiling," said Jules.

"No time. Can you locate the brains?" asked Jake.

Gottlieb zoomed in on the mega-Kaiju's head. It bristled with bony spikes and crests that protected the skull. "Hostile's central brain mass is heavily armored. Your weapons won't be able to penetrate."

Nate realized where Jake was going with this. "What about a *secondary* brain?" he asked.

Gottlieb worked the holo screen. Three areas lit up in the mega-Kaiju's hindquarters near the monster's tails.

"Hostile has *three* secondary brains. One for each component Kaiju," said Gottlieb.

Gipsy Avenger flexed her arms and dashed through the city. FHOOM! Twin forearm plasma chain saws whipped out, courtesy of Obsidian Fury.

Gipsy kicked off from a building and soared into the air. She slashed the mega-Kaiju across the back!

The mega-Kaiju turned to attack Gipsy. But Saber Athena flipped over the behemoth and slashed it with her sword.

The mega-Kaiju raised a giant claw to smash Saber Athena, but then Bracer Phoenix attacked it from behind with missiles. Bracer threw his morning star hand. The spikes on the giant weapon rotated quickly and then smashed the mega-Kaiju in the face. The blow broke off one of its mandible tusks.

Amara and Jinhai retracted the morning star and leapt into the air to attack the mega-Kaiju's secondary brains, which were inside the monster's back. The mega-Kaiju spun around and swatted Bracer in midair, which sent the Jaeger flying.

The entire group strained in their conn-pods as they battled the mega-Kaiju.

Then it suddenly lashed out at Saber Athena, ripping both the Jaeger's legs off. Saber tried to crawl away, but mega-Kaiju shot its double tail out like a scorpion and pinned the crippled Jaeger to the ground. Then, it tossed her aside.

Renata and Ryoichi grimaced in agony as the biofeedback of the Jaeger death surged through them.

But the distraction gave Gipsy an opening to strike deep into the beast with both plasma chain saws. Gipsy took out one of the secondary brains! The war room erupted in cheers.

The mega-Kaiju screeched as a section of its flank went dead. The strain from the deadweight tore apart the ripper sutures. The mechanical monsters tumbled to the ground—most were destroyed in the process. Jake's plan was working!

"One down, two to go," said Jake over the comms.

Suddenly, Gipsy Avenger was slammed backward as the mega-Kaiju snapped off one of her plasma chain saws. Gipsy flew across the city and went down hard.

Bracer Phoenix circled the mega-Kaiju. Amara and Jinhai pressed forward to attack while Vik viciously worked her rail gun.

"I can't punch through!" said Vik.

On the display, Jinhai spotted a spire atop a neighboring building.

"Target that spire! I'm gonna try something!" said Jinhai.

Vik's rail gun sheared the spire off the building. Bracer Phoenix ran, leapt, and caught the spire as it fell. Then it slammed the spire deep into the mega-Kaiju's flesh.

Amara completed the move with a holographic spire. Another secondary brain faded out.

The mega-Kaiju bellowed. It whipped around and snatched Bracer Phoenix up in its jaws. The conn-pods started to break apart!

"All pilots, eject! Eject!" said Jinhai.

Amara, Jinhai, and Vik's escape pods blasted free just as Bracer Phoenix was crushed between the mega-Kaiju's jaws.

Amara's escape pod smoked as it landed roughly on the ground. She managed to scramble out just before the mega-Kaiju thundered past and crushed the pod.

She turned to see Jinhai rushing up to her with a bloodied Vik.

The mega-Kaiju thundered toward Mount Fuji. Then out of nowhere, Gipsy Avenger appeared. The Jaeger jumped on the mega-Kaiju's back.

The two wrestled. Then the mega-Kaiju got the upper hand. It rose, grabbed Gipsy, and dragged her across the pavement.

Gipsy fired her plasma cannon and blasted it at the beast. The mega-Kaiju roared in pain and anger and lashed out with its tail.

The tail slammed through Gipsy's conn-pod. It tore up the back wall. Nate grunted in pain as the tail punctured his side.

"Nate! C'mon, stay with me, brother—" said Jake.

Nate tried to maintain control, but he lost consciousness.

Jules's heart leapt into her throat as she viewed Nate's fluctuating vital signs on her holo screen. "Warning. Neural handshake lost," said the computer.

Jake grimaced as he suddenly absorbed the double neural load of piloting Gipsy solo.

The mega-Kaiju slammed Gipsy Avenger aside. Then, it roared in triumph.

"Yes! Oh! Get up from *that*, you pile of junk," said Newt, watching.

Newt stiffened as the mega-Kaiju noticed him. The giant beast came face-to-face with the tiny human. Sniffed. Then turned away, lumbering toward Mount Fuji. Newt chuckled in relief.

"Bye!" he said.

15

"Shao? Is there anything you can do to help?" asked Gottlieb desperately.

"I need more time!" she replied.

"We don't have any. If the hostile reaches Mount Fuji—" Gottlieb's voice weakened.

Then Jake's voice came over the comms! "Gipsy to Command," he said. "I'm not going to let that happen."

Jake strained to get Gipsy to her feet. His nose started to bleed from the neural strain of piloting the Jaeger alone. He was going to stop Raijin or die trying!

"Jake, you can't operate Gipsy without a copilot," said Gottlieb.

"Gipsy Avenger. This is Amara Namani. Stand by for assist!" said Amara over the comms.

Amara sprinted across the roof of a partially destroyed building. Gipsy Avenger staggered to one knee right beside the building, giving Jake a clear view of what Amara was about to attempt.

"Amara, don't! You won't make it!" he screamed.

"I'm gonna." Amara sprinted to the edge.

"Don't!" yelled Jake.

"Gonna!" said Amara.

She leapt off the roof, aiming for Gipsy Avenger's head, but fell painfully short and plummeted toward the ground.

Gipsy Avenger whirled and just barely caught her in the palm of its massive hand. Gipsy Avenger raised Amara up to her ripped-open faceplate.

Amara scrambled into the conn-pod. Jake shot her a look that was half rebuke and half admiration.

"Told you," said Jake.

"Since when do I listen?" asked Amara.

Nate grimaced. He was barely clinging to consciousness. "Amara . . . you're up," he said, smiling. Then, he winced in pain. Amara rushed to his side and initialized the ejection sequence.

"What are you doing?" Jake asked Nate.

"Getting out of the way," Nate grimaced. "Glad it's you. You're crazy enough to kick that thing's butt."

Jake nodded. His friend's words gave him strength.

Amara punched the final command. "Ejection sequence

initiated," said a computer voice. Nate was ejected from Gipsy Avenger via an escape pod.

Amara climbed into Nate's now-empty drift cradle.

"You ready for this, smallie?" asked Jake.

Amara finished locking herself into the cradle. "One way to find out," she said.

Jake frowned, but he fired up the controls. "Stand by, Command. Initiating neural handshake . . ."

Gipsy Avenger was still on one knee among the debris, as beaten up as the wrecked city around her. A beat passed and nothing happened.

Then suddenly, WHOOM! Gipsy Avenger surged to her feet, rising from the ashes. Gipsy slammed her fist into her palm. She was ready.

WHAM! Gipsy's right leg buckled. It was severely damaged from her battle with the mega-Kaiju. The Jaeger crashed back to one knee.

Alarms wailed. Amara frantically punched holo commands.

"WARNING. CASCADE FAILURE. MULTIPLE SYSTEMS," said a computer voice.

"Reboot!" screamed Jake.

"I'm trying!" said Amara.

Gottlieb tensed. He tracked the mega-Kaiju's position. "The hostile is two kilometers from the summit of Mount Fuji!"

Trees toppled as the mega-Kaiju thundered forward. The beast was wounded but determined. The snowcapped summit of Mount Fuji glistened in the distance.

Amara frantically tried to reboot Gipsy's systems.

Jake spoke into the comms: "Gottlieb, is there enough fuel left in any of your thrusters to get us into the atmosphere?"

"The atmosphere?" said Gottlieb. He punched commands into the computer. "Possibly, but there won't be enough to slow your reentry."

"Not going to slow down. We'll come in hot and drop Gipsy right on top of that thing," said Jake. Then he looked at Amara. "We'll use my escape pod, smallie."

Gottlieb worked his data pad. "Jake, there's only one thruster pod with enough fuel remaining to reach the troposphere. Sending location . . ."

The intel popped up on the holo screens. Amara stiffened. "It's too far away. We're not gonna make it."

Then, Shao's voice came over the comms: "Gipsy Avenger—my systems are online!"

A familiar, brightly colored holo display flared to life and a message flashed across it: REMOTE UPLINK ACTIVE. "Sending help!" said Shao.

The cargo doors of a heavy-lift Shao V-Dragon opened. Something rolled out of the back and unfurled in midair, the sun flaring behind it.

"Scrapper!" Amara exclaimed. It was her Jaeger!

Scrapper curled into a ball in midair, smashed through a building, and landed on the ground in one sleek movement.

This was what Shao had been working on! She had been modifying Scrapper's conn-pod rings to remotely operate the Jaeger from the Shatterdome.

A Shao data core sat where the pilot rings used to be. That's how Shao was remotely operating Scrapper! Her holo screen locked onto a thruster pod.

"I've located the thruster pod! Stand by," she exclaimed.

The air was thick from all the destruction.

WHOOSH! Scrapper surged out, with the thruster pod slung across her back.

Jake and Amara watched Scrapper closing in with the thruster pod through Gipsy's destroyed face shield. Amara punched commands, doing quick calculations.

"Thrust is too strong. We won't be able to hold on to it," said Amara.

"I upgraded Scrapper's weapons. I can weld the thruster to your hand," said Shao.

"Nice!" said Amara.

Scrapper tossed the thruster pod down, and Gipsy reached out and grabbed it!

Plasma blasters with Shao Industries markings sprang from Scrapper's shoulders. Metal sizzled as Scrapper scrambled onto Gipsy's arm, using the blasters to weld the thruster pod to Gipsy's hand.

"We'll only get one shot at this," said Amara.

"Then we better make it count," said Jake.

KA-THOOM! Scrapper's blasters accidentally ignited the thruster pod. Gipsy surged forward, careening out of control. Jake and Amara were slammed hard.

Shock spread across Shao's face. The remote conn-rings shuddered from the uplink feedback. "Ignition! We have ignition!" she said.

Gipsy blasted horizontally through the city, tearing up the street and scraping buildings in its path. The Jaeger was completely out of control!

Scrapper tumbled. The little Jaeger's foot got caught on Gipsy's rear fin.

Gipsy careened through the city and then started to climb into the air. Scrapper flailed—unexpectedly along for the ride.

"I'm stuck!" said Shao, who was remotely operating Scrapper.

Jake and Amara struggled to adjust their trajectory. "Stay there," said Jake to Shao. "You're an extra ton we can drop on that thing."

Gipsy Avenger burst through the clouds. They were headed for the upper atmosphere now. Pieces of the battle-damaged Jaeger were ripped off by extreme forces.

Warning alarms wailed. The conn-pod shook and threatened to disintegrate.

"She's coming apart!" said Amara.

"Almost there!" said Jake.

The thruster pod flamed out. Its fuel was spent. Gipsy reached the apex of her trajectory. Gravity momentarily ceased to exist. Jake and Amara floated into the air. Then, Gipsy started to plummet. They were headed back down!

Jake and Amara were slammed hard as Gipsy plummeted back to earth. A holo screen flashed. "We're locked on target!" said Amara.

"Get out of there! Eject!" said Gottlieb over the comms.

"We're drifting off course," said Jake.

Amara thought fast. "Use the plasma cannon!" she shouted.

Jake grinned and punched the commands. "Disengaging safety protocols!" he said.

Gipsy's plasma cannon fired. The continuous stream of energy began to correct the Jaeger's course, but Gipsy's arm started to glow from the intense heat. Pieces started to break off.

Jake and Amara struggled to maintain control. Warning alarms wailed. "Warning. Exceeding structural limits!" said a computer voice.

The plasma cannon flared out. It took a hunk of Gipsy's forearm with it.

Gipsy shuddered. Alarms wailed. Jake threw a worried look at Amara. Were they going to make it?

Amara punched holo commands. A reticle adjusted and locked onto the mega-Kaiju on the side of Mount Fuji.

"Target locked!" said Amara.

Gottlieb eyed the rate of Gipsy's descent. "Jake! Amara! You need to eject!" he said.

Gipsy screamed toward earth. At this point, it was glowing from the friction of reentry. Pieces were still falling off. Wind slammed through Gipsy's destroyed face shield. Flames ignited just outside!

"Disconnect!" Jake screamed at Amara.

Amara froze, terrified. Jake stretched out his hand. "It's okay! I got you!" he said.

Amara swallowed the fear and punched a holo command. The drift cradle disconnected from her drivesuit. Amara leapt for Jake, fighting the howling wind. Jake barely snagged her hand.

He pulled Amara close. She clung to him, heart racing.

Jake grinned and punched holo commands. "Gipsy to Command. We are getting the hell out of here."

"Warning. Escape pod inoperable. Warning," said a computer voice.

Gipsy plummeted like a skyscraper dropped from space.

Jake eyed a holo indicator counting down the kilometers to impact. It was moving fast! He looked at Amara, eyes filled with the knowledge of their impending death.

"I'm sorry, smallie," said Jake.

Amara pushed her fear aside and mustered a smile. "For what? We got to save the world. Your dad would be proud."

Jake nodded. The sentiment hit him hard.

ZZZTTTTTT! A plasma beam interrupted the moment as it cut into the conn-pod behind them. They whirled in surprise.

Scrapper was using her plasma blasters to cut a hole in the back of Gipsy's head! The little Jaeger made it into the conn-pod. "You guys need a lift?" asked Shao, her voice coming over the remote link. Jake and Amara felt relief pulse through them.

"Twenty kilometers to impact! Get out of there!" said Gottlieb.

Jake and Amara scrambled into Scrapper. Amara dove into one of the counterbalance ear alcoves and Jake dove into the other.

The mega-Kaiju thundered up the side of Mount Fuji. It reached the snowcapped crater at the summit. It roared, about to leap in and start the world-ending chain reaction. But then, it paused. A sound drew its attention to Gipsy Avenger hurtling toward it.

"Hang on!" said Jake.

"I am hanging on!" said Amara.

"Hang tighter!" said Jake.

Scrapper jumped off Gipsy and then curled into a ball just as the Jaeger slammed into the mega-Kaiju. The impact went off like an atomic bomb. Scrapper bounced and careened off trees. Then she unfurled as the shock wave hit her. Jake and Amara were thrown hard by the blast!

The mega-Kaiju slid to a stop. It was smoking and damaged. It started to rise, but then it collapsed. Its skin had been torn apart and smeared across several miles of Mount Fuji—all that was left of it was its head and upper body.

The mega-Kaiju's locator dot winked out on the holo screen. The war room techs cheered! Jules smiled, but she was still worried about Nate. Gottlieb sighed in relief. The end of the world came a little too close this time.

Shao beamed. She was exhausted but triumphant.

Jinhai, Vik, Ryoichi, Renata, and an injured-but-standing

Ilya cheered. It was a costly victory, but the Jaegers and their pilots had saved the world once again!

Above Tokyo, Newt seethed at his loss.

"All right. Okay. Sure. Plan B then. Always a plan B," he muttered. He turned to escape to his V-Dragon and WHAM! A fist cracked him in the face and knocked him out. It was Nate! He was worse for the wear but still on his feet. He grimaced from the effort and growled at Newt, who was now laid out on the ground.

"That's about enough of that," said Nate. He activated his comm. "Command, this is Lambert."

Jules exhaled in relief at the sound of Nate's voice.

"Be advised, I just caught us a Newt."

At Mount Fuji, snow continued to fall, creating a surreal winter scene. Jake and Amara were walking away from Scrapper, who was splayed out in the background. The little Jaeger was damaged from the force of the blast.

"Copy that, Nate. Good to hear you're still with us," said Jake.

"You, too, brother. Knew you could do it," said Nate.

"I had a lot of help," said Jake. He grinned at Amara as he pulled his helmet off.

"Nice work, Ranger Namani," said Nate. Amara smiled.

"I've never seen snow before," she said to Jake.

"Yeah . . . almost makes you forget the giant dead monster over there," he teased.

"I feel like you're about to make another one of your big dumb speeches," said Amara.

"Dumb? That speech was inspirational. It literally saved the world."

Jake nailed Amara with a snowball. She shrieked and threw one back.

"Wait. Did everyone really think it was dumb?" asked Jake.

Amara just laughed. She looked up as the sun set over Mount Fuji. The dead mega-Kaiju's tattered body hung off it in the distance. Snow glistened in every direction, and at that moment, she felt happy to be alive.